MAX DEVEREAUX

BERNADETTE MARIE

5 PRINCE PUBLISHING

Published by 5 PRINCE PUBLISHING & BOOKS, LLC

PO Box 865, Arvada, CO 80001

www.5PrinceBooks.com

Digital ISBN: 978-1-63112-256-9

Print ISBN: 9978-1-63112-264-4

Cover Credit: Marianne Nowicki

For Stan
I'll always be grateful that after navigating long distance we were able
to follow each other
here and there.
I love you.

ACKNOWLEDGMENTS

TNGSJ, I hope you always follow your dreams! And I hope I always remember your faces.

Mom and Sissy, We certainly call the shots now, don't we?!

Cate, Therapy comes in weird ways. Thanks for your insight, your comments, and your friendship.

My Book Hive, I'm grateful that you are all on this journey with me.

To My Readers, I love bringing you new families to immerse yourself in.

MAX DEVEREAUX

The orange Home Depot bucket full of tools was balanced on the tailgate of Max's Ford F-150. He fastened his tool belt, and then took a sip of coffee from his travel mug.

His morning ritual had always been a hot cup of coffee he brewed himself, country music on his radio, and the sunrise out his window as he drove to his construction sites and checked on their progress. He was still finishing a remodel on his brother's house, and he'd be done with that within the week.

His brother and sister-in-law had wanted a master bathroom added to the house, as well as a little more space, now that they had their baby. Max's niece was almost six months old, and the house was looking amazing, he thought.

Lifting the bucket off the truck and lowering it to the ground, Max pushed up the tailgate and locked it. He'd had enough tools stolen over the years, it was worth the thirty seconds to lock everything up tight each time.

As he turned to walk up toward the house, a car pulled up behind him, so he stopped. It was then he noticed the sparkle of the bracelet on the wrist of the driver. The hand holding his cup of coffee began to tremble, and the bucket started to slip from his grasp.

Instead of dropping the tools to the ground, he set the bucket down and waited for the driver to step out of the car.

The moment he saw her, his tongue swelled in his mouth and his heart rate kicked up to an uncomfortable pace.

"Good morning, Max," her voice was soft and gentle, just like she was.

"Meghann," he said, surprised he could even get that out. "What are you doing here?"

She stayed safely behind her car door. "I hope you don't mind. Paige told me where to find you. I took her yoga class this morning." As she moved away from the car he noticed the outfit she wore. Yoga pants and some fitted top that hugged her beautiful body.

"What are you doing back here? Aren't you still filming your show?"

"It's on break," she said, warily inching toward him. "Listen, I was hoping to talk to you about a job."

Max took another sip of his coffee, nearly choking on its bitter taste. "What kind of job?"

"My brother and I want to have some work done on our mom's house. She's recently been diagnosed with Alzheimer's and her house needs updating and some safety features added."

Max took a step toward her and reached for her hand. "I'm so sorry to hear about your mom. I should have kept in touch with her."

"That's why we came looking for you. She always loved you, so she'd be comfortable with you in her house."

"How soon are you looking at starting this?"

"As soon as you can. She's walking with a walker, and her bathroom has to be fitted. The kitchen is old and..."

He gave her hand a squeeze. "You can walk me through it later. Of course I'll do that for you."

He noticed the curtains in the front window moving, and he assumed that they were being watched.

Meghann must have noticed too. "I should let you go. I think your client is waiting for you."

Still holding her hand, he gazed into dark eyes that he'd missed. "Would you like to see those clients? They have someone special in there."

"Whose house is this?"

"Chase and Hillary's."

Her eyes went wide. "Chase and Hillary are married?"

He chuckled. That was a common reaction to his brother marrying his sister's best friend. "Not only are they married; they have a baby."

Meghann raised her other hand to her heart. "I can't even believe it."

Neither could he. "Would you like to say hello?"

"I would."

Max let go of her hand and picked up his bucket. They headed toward the front door as it opened. Hillary stepped out with his niece Kennedy on her hip.

"Oh, look who is in town," she squealed. She reached out an arm to hug Meghann as Kennedy took a handful of her hair. "I'm sorry," Hillary said, taking her daughter's hand and releasing the hair.

"I can't believe you and Chase have a baby."

Hillary kissed her daughter on the head. "Neither can I. More surprising is that he's an amazing and attentive father."

Max nodded. "I have to agree. Who would have thought Chase had it in him?"

Meghann laughed. "I should let Max get to work."

Hillary shook her head. "Do you have time for a cup of coffee? I'd love to catch up."

"Can I take a raincheck? I need to get back to my mom. I'll be in town for the week at least. I'd love to see everyone."

Max bit down on the inside of his cheek. One week. His heart was going to ache that entire time, but she needed him, so he'd be there for her.

"Your number is still the same?" he asked as she turned to walk back toward her car.

Meghann stopped and looked up at him. "Yes."

"I'll call you and make plans to come look at the house."

"I really appreciate that."

Max watched her walk back to her car and drive away.

"Are you going to be able to function?" Hillary asked, and he shifted his attention back to her as he stepped through the front door.

"I'm fine."

"You didn't know she was in town, did you?"

"I did not. Seems as if Paige did."

"She mentioned it."

Max walked toward the bathroom he'd been working on. "No one thought to mention it to me?"

Hillary followed him. "You get a little worked up over her."

"Exactly why I think it would be nice to know she might drive up on me."

"It's not all bad, is it?"

Max set his bucket on the floor. "No, it's never bad. We parted on good terms. I'd have been miserable in New York, and she wouldn't have what she has, had she stayed. We're not compatible, but we can be friendly."

"What did she want to talk to you about?"

Max leaned up against the doorjamb. "Her mother's got Alzheimer's."

"Oh, that sucks."

"Ya. Well they want to do some remodeling on her house to help her out."

"And they want you to do it?"

He chuckled. "She would be comfortable with me in the house."

Hillary hitched Kennedy up on her hip. "She trusts you, Max. She knows you'll always be there for her."

And didn't he know it? It's what made getting over her so damn hard.

CHAPTER 2

By lunch time, and nap time for little Kennedy, Max wrapped up the grout work in the bathroom and packed up his truck.

He sat on the street for a few minutes contemplating his next move. With a few deep breaths, he dialed Meghann's phone number, still having committed it to memory, even though he'd taken it out of his contact list.

"Hi, Max," she answered on the other end, which meant he still came up on her phone. He wasn't sure what to think of that.

"Hey. I just finished up at my brother's for the day. Would it be a good time to come by and look at your mom's house?"

She hesitated for a moment. "We're having a really hard day, but her PT is here, and that usually wears her out. Maybe she'll lay down for a nap."

"I can come some other—"

"No. Come now. And, Max, thanks for taking a look. I know this puts you in an awkward position."

At least she was aware of it. "Your mom has always been good to me. If I can make her life more comfortable with my skills, then I'm happy to do it." And he meant it. No one should have to suffer through something like that, especially Patricia Carr.

"I appreciate it. I'll see you shortly," she said and the call was disconnected.

Max sat there for another moment. He had a few more stops before he headed over to the house.

THERE WAS one particular street in Olde Town that Max knew well. His sister had built her business as a fashion consultant and jewelry designer in her store *Kennedy Devereaux Designs*. Her husband was one of the four men that had opened the *Kingsley Tap House* next door. Max's brother, Chase, rented an office for *Devereaux Limousine* just a block over, and Paige taught yoga at the wellness center at the end of the building. In the center of the group of shops, there was a florist. He wanted to get flowers for Meghann's mother, in case she was awake. Perhaps it would ease him into the house. By chance, he noted that Paige's car was parked in the lot. He'd like to have a few words with her too.

Ten minutes after parking, he walked through the front door of the wellness center with a bouquet of roses. Paige looked up at him and smiled.

"Those aren't for me, are they?"

"Like hell," his comment was harsh.

"Well excuse me. What's up your ass?" she asked as she mopped the floor in the yoga studio.

"Don't you think it's worth mentioning to me that my ex-fiancée is in town?"

The anger cooled from her eyes and she grinned. "I take it you ran into Meghann?"

"Yeah. She showed up at Chase and Hillary's house this morning. She said she'd taken your class."

"She did. And damn, she's still one of the best students I've ever had."

Max let out a low growl. "You could have told me she was here."

"I'm sorry. Max, Meghann is here."

"You're a snot."

"Never claimed not to be. What did she want?"

Max ran his free hand over the back of his neck. "Her mom has Alzheimer's, and she and her brother want me to fix up her house to accommodate her as it progresses."

Paige pressed her hand to her chest. "That breaks my heart."

"Yeah. She thinks that if I'm in the house, her mom will be more at ease."

"She always did like you."

And that was part of what made Meghann's exit so hard. "I'm headed over there now."

"I'm sorry I didn't tell you," her voice had softened.

"Don't think I'm done busting your chops over it."

"I'd be disappointed if you just let it go. That's not your style," she said as Max turned and walked out.

He wasn't sure he liked that comment any more than her not telling him that Meghann was in town. But, actions spoke rather loudly, and Max was one to hold on to things like grudges... and feelings for people.

MEGHANN and her brother Ryan watched the physical therapist work with their mother. The woman who would visit twice a week had a gentle and soothing way that seemed to keep their mother calm, and willing to work.

"I think she's looking better, don't you?" Ryan asked.

Meghann turned her gaze to him. "You have to realize that when I last visited, she was perfectly normal. No, I don't think she looks better at all."

"Well, you don't see her every day. I think she's getting stronger."

Meghann batted away tears that had pooled in her eyes. "Was that a dig at me being gone?"

"It doesn't help, that's for damn sure."

"I have a job, and it's not here."

"Well noted," he said as he retreated to the kitchen and Meghann followed.

"Listen, I appreciate that you're here and that you take care of her. I came when you said to come."

"And you'll leave, too."

"I have a life I'm committed to."

"You mean you have a contract that commits you. I have no doubt if it weren't for millions of someone else's dollars, you'd be here. You'd be married and you'd probably have a house full of kids. But instead, you chose corporate dollars and your face on some TV screen."

That comment socked her right in the gut. She didn't even have a rebuttal for it because it was true. Her success came at the price others were willing to pay for her. But it didn't mean she didn't love her family and want to be there, or that she'd forgotten just what she'd given up with Max to live out her dream.

CHAPTER 3

Max drove slowly from Olde Town to the west side of the city. He made sure he hit all the lights he could, drove just at the speed limit, and might have missed the turn on purpose, but then again he might have just had his mind occupied.

The roses for Meghann's mother rode next to him in the passenger seat. What if she didn't know him? He should be the last person she'd remember, and that was okay, but it still freaked him out.

He pulled up in front of the house where Meghann and Ryan had grown up. Max had spent a lot of time in that house over the years. Barbecues, parties, Christmases, and Sunday dinners. Meghann's father had passed from cancer shortly before she'd left for New York, which had only made her decision to leave them all behind that much harder on her.

Max stepped out of his truck and took the bouquet with him. Ryan opened the door before he even made it to the front porch.

"You didn't have to bring me flowers," he joked as he moved in to give Max a hug that ended with a slap on the shoulder.

"I brought them for your mom. I thought she'd appreciate them since I'm a stranger in her house."

Ryan narrowed his eyes on him. "You're no stranger. You were like a son to her."

"I haven't seen her in years."

"Well, I'm not saying she won't have forgotten you, but she'll know you're like family."

Ryan opened the front door and Max walked through. Meghann headed toward them from the hallway where she'd closed the door behind her.

"Mom laid down." She looked at the flowers that Max carried.

"These are for your mom. I wanted her to be impressed by me, I guess."

The smile that formed on Meghann's lips was soft and sweet, just as he'd remembered. "She was always impressed by you." Meghann reached for the flowers. "Let me put them in some water."

They walked back to the kitchen and it did Max's heart good to see that nothing had changed in all the years since he'd been there. There was comfort in that, he thought.

"Looks just as I remember it," he said.

Meghann set the flowers on the kitchen table and pulled a vase out of the cabinet. "After Dad died, Mom didn't want to change anything. Almost as if she thought he'd come back and need to find it again."

Ryan leaned up against the counter. "Doesn't make sense, if you ask me. She should have had new appliances, updated cabinets, and something that reflected her style."

"I see it all the time," Max said. "There is comfort in a home never changing."

Ryan looked at his watch. "Well, it's going to have to change a bit to keep her safe. That's the main focus here."

"We can do that. Do you guys want to walk me through it?"

Ryan moved to him and held out his hand. "I have to get to

work. Meg knows everything. We've talked in great length about it and we know you're our guy. So don't take advantage of us," he joked and Max, shaking Ryan's hand, wondered if he'd flinched at Ryan's humor. Surely he knew Max would never do such a thing.

"I'll take good care of your mom."

"I know you will." Ryan headed toward the back door. "I'll be back at six, sis. Call if you need anything."

And a moment later, they were alone.

Meghann filled the vase with water, and turned back to the table to set the flowers in it. "She'll love these."

"I remembered she liked roses."

"Twenty bushes still in the back yard, though I'm thinking we might have to pull some of those out. She can't keep up with them."

He noticed the tears in her eyes as she wiped them away. It was instinct to move to her and pull her into his arms. Five years might have passed between them, and he might have avoided watching TV so that he didn't see her, but he couldn't bear to see her hurt.

"Hey," Max said softly as he ran his hand down her hair. "It's okay."

Meghann's face pressed into his chest and he inhaled the familiar scent of her shampoo as she sobbed against him.

Max held her against him until her breath steadied. When she eased back slightly to look up at him, he kept his arms in place.

"I'm glad you're here," she said pressing her hands to his chest. "I want to make sure everything is easier for her."

"I'm here to help you do that, down to the bushes in the back. I'll make sure they're taken care of through the summer."

She eased back a little further. "You're a gardener now?"

"I'm a friend, Meg." He stopped short of telling her *I'd do anything for you.*

Max let his arms drop as Meghann took a step back.

She walked to the counter and tore off a piece of paper towel to wipe the tears from her eyes. Meghann took a moment to compose herself, drawing in a long breath before she turned around.

"Let me show you around. I suppose most of the things aren't construction based, but—"

"But I'll do them anyway, Meg. Tell me what you need."

Max pulled out the small notebook he kept in his back pocket to take notes. He saw her grin when he did so. When they'd lived together, years ago, how many times had she accidentally washed the notebooks he'd forgotten to take out of his pockets?

Meghann walked him through the improvements improvements they wanted such as new railings and toilets in the bathroom along with fixing the flooring in the hallway and living room. The back patio would need to be replaced, and she stressed that it was important since her mother enjoyed spending hours outside looking over her rose bushes. The fence around the house needed to be replaced so that the gate would effectively keep Meghann's mother in the yard, and not walking out onto the street.

Max followed her through the house taking notes and making plans in his head.

"So, what do you think? Are you willing to do something little like this?"

Max closed his notebook and tucked it back in his pocket. "It's not little, Meg. It's a big deal to keep a wonderful woman safe. Consider it a top priority for me."

Meghann reached for his hand and gave it a squeeze. "You can't imagine what this means to me."

The question on the tip of his tongue was to ask her when she'd be leaving again. He just wanted to prepare himself for her departure. In five years, he hadn't spoken to her more than three times. Already he'd touched her and held her. It was going to hurt to let her go again, even if he thought he was ready for it.

"Max Devereaux, you came for dinner after all." Patricia Carr walked down the hallway slowly toward him.

Max shifted a glance toward Meghann, and then lifted a smile toward Patricia.

"Dinner?"

"Yes, you didn't forget did you? We were going to talk about your engagement dinner," Patricia continued. "I don't like those chicken meals at the hotels."

"Mom," Meghann began and Max reached for her hand and gave it a squeeze.

"I have to get back to work right now. How about I bring dinner back by in a few hours. Do you still enjoy those ribs from Franks?"

"You know I do. I'll see you later," she smiled at him as if she'd talked to him every day, and passed by to head to the kitchen.

"Max, we can't let her think—"

"We can until dinner. I know that I might come back for dinner and she won't know me at all. I understand that. So what did that hurt for the moment?"

"You've always been so good to me."

He smiled through the pain of it, holding in what he'd wanted to say. *But you left anyway.*

CHAPTER 4

Meghann watched as Max pulled away from the house before walking back to the kitchen where her mother filled the tea kettle and set it on the stove. Maybe she'd buy her one of those instant hot water kettles so that she wouldn't use the stove as much.

"Max brought you roses," she said, pointing to the vase on the table.

"He's my favorite, well aside from you and Ryan, of course."

"So you remember him?"

Her mother laughed as she pulled two mugs from the cupboard. "Meghann, what kind of question is that? Of course I remember him. You live with him. You're getting married. I'm expecting grandkids," she said with a wide smile.

What was Meghann supposed to do when her mother talked like this? Was Max right? Was it okay to just go with what she was thinking?

Perhaps for now, she'd steer around the conversation. "We could work on that puzzle some more, when you're done with your tea. We made a lot of progress yesterday."

Her mother drew her brows together. "What puzzle? Who is

making tea?" Meghann noticed her mother wring her hands as if to keep them occupied.

Meghann pointed to the stove and her mother's eyes widened.

"I'm making tea?" She stared at the kettle for a moment, her hands stilled, and her brows furrowed as if she were trying to remember. "I'm making tea."

Meghann was for sure going out to buy her a kettle as soon as she could. Maybe she'd even unplug the stove so that her mother would just assume it was broken.

Again, her mother wrung her hands. "Sorry, sweetheart. I forget things." The words were sharp, and she knew her mother was irritated that she couldn't recall what she'd just been doing.

"I know, Mama. Can I help you finish this off?"

Her mother smiled briefly at her, and sat down at the table. "I enjoy having you here. I know that you had to travel here. I can't remember where you live."

The tides were turning again, she thought. "I live in New York, Mama."

"Right. You have a cooking show."

Meghann smiled as she pulled the whistling pot from the stovetop and carried it to the table. "That's right."

"See, I know things."

"You do. Sometimes it just gets jumbled up."

Her mother watched her pour the water into the mug and carry the kettle back to the stove. "Where did these roses come from?" her mother asked.

Meghann drew in a deep breath. "Max brought those to you."

"I don't know a Max."

Tears began to sting Meghann's eyes. How was she going to be able to leave her again?

"Max is a friend of mine. He's going to do some work in the house to make it safer."

"I don't want anyone in the house. I don't trust anyone."

"You trust Max."

Her mother took a paper napkin from the holder and began to tear it into pieces. "Meghann, did I forget I know Max?"

Meghann took her mother's hand. "Yes. You just forgot. I was engaged to him, but I moved to New York and he stayed here."

Her mother nodded slowly, taking it in. "I forget sometimes."

"You do, but that's okay. Ryan and I will be here to help you."

"Max?" she said his name again. "I'll try to remember Max."

"Would you like to see a picture of him? He's bringing dinner tonight for you."

"For me?"

"Well, for us. He's bringing ribs."

"From Frank's?"

That she remembered? "Yes. You like Frank's."

"I do. It's my favorite."

"He knew that. And he knows you love roses, too."

Her mother touched the petal of one of the roses in the vase. "I do love roses. Max sounds like a nice man. Did you say you were marrying him?"

Meghann was growing tired with the conversation. She wasn't equipped to handle what was happening with her mother. "Yes, Mama."

AFTER MAX HAD CHECKED in on the other build sites and put out a few fires, so to speak, he headed back to his office and shut the door.

He dropped his clipboard of notes for the next day on the desk and fell into his chair. Pulling the notebook out of his pocket, he looked at the few items he'd jotted down for Patricia Carr's house.

Curiosity got the better of him, so he googled Alzheimer's to see what kinds of things happen to a person when they suffer from the disease.

As he read, he grew more depressed, seeing the changes that Patricia might be going through.

What was Patricia going to do when Meghann went back to New York?

And Ryan couldn't be with his mother all the time. He had his own job too, and it wasn't one that offered a lot of free time. Ryan Carr was a veterinarian and ran a hospital for animals. Things came up, and he'd be pulled away from home.

Would Patricia be better in a home, he wondered?

No, he thought. If he were suffering from something like this, he'd want to be where it was familiar too.

That thought led to the next one. What could he do to the house to make it more functional but not uncomfortable? Would he only be able to work on days where she remembered him? Would she always remember him? Would her course of this disease only be physical?

But then he thought of what she'd said to them. In her mind, it was still five years ago. She thought they were still engaged and Meghann was still home.

Max sat back in his chair and linked his fingers behind his head.

He thought of his own father, who had recently moved to Florida to live with a woman he'd met on a cruise. What if something like this happened to him in Florida? How would they ever get him home if he didn't recognize his children.

The very thought sickened him.

He looked up at the clock on the wall. His brother-in-law had given it to him for Christmas. It had the *Kingsley Tap House* logo on it. But it told him he needed to go get dinner and head back to Patricia Carr's house.

Would she remember him when he arrived?

CHAPTER 5

Armed with bags of barbecue, slaw, potato salad, and brownies for dessert, Max stood on the front porch and rang the doorbell.

The lights were on in the house, and he heard the TV from inside, but no one seemed to hear him ringing the doorbell. So he did it again.

When no one came to the door he stepped back and looked at the house. No windows were open for him to yell into. He walked to the side of the house where the small gate opened to the back yard. It was one of the things on his list from Meghann that would have to be fixed. Sure enough, he easily opened it and walked into the yard. Patricia wouldn't have any problem doing the same and getting away.

He heard talking as he turned the corner. Meghann and Patricia were tending to her roses.

"Hi, ladies. It's a nice night for a picnic," he said, but wondered if it was the wrong thing to do when Meghann's head popped up and her eyes narrowed on him.

Patricia, however, turned toward him in her big brimmed hat and smiled. "Oh, doesn't that sound lovely. Max, I didn't know you were coming or I'd have made up some tea. You love iced tea."

The narrow stare Meghann was giving him softened and she looked at her mother. "You remember he likes iced tea?"

"Of course. He comes over all the time and we have tea on the back patio. Your father mows the lawn while we talk."

"Max," Patricia walked toward him, a rose held in her gloved hand. "Let's set up on the patio. I have some nice Tupperware plates I bought at a party not too long ago. Sheila Waxer was having a party, and she expected everyone to buy something. Oh, she's such a busybody," Patricia continued as she walked into the house, though there was a hint of panic in her eyes, and he couldn't imagine what was going on in her head.

Meghann moved to him. "She's all over the place today."

"Sheila Waxer died when we were ten," he noted.

"Yeah, and my dad has been gone for five years."

Meghann brushed her hand over her cheek, and Max noticed it left a trail of dirt. Cautiously he lifted his hand to brush it away. Meghann flinched at first, but then let him touch her.

"All gone."

"Thank you," she said looking toward the back door. "She didn't remember you after you'd left today, when I told her you brought her roses."

"That's sad. I was hoping I was the breakthrough."

"She worked to remember your name, because she knows she forgets things. But then it all changes and she could tell me we were getting married. I just agreed with her because I knew she'd forget anyway."

Max wasn't sure how to take that, but he wasn't going to bring it up.

"Why don't we eat dinner and see how it goes. Any rules?"

"I took your suggestion, and today I just went with whatever she was thinking."

"Got it. So if she doesn't know me, I introduce myself. If she thinks we're getting married, then we are."

Meghann bit down on her lip. "I guess so. Ryan should be here soon."

Max followed Meghann into the house with the bag of food. When they got there, Patricia was standing in the kitchen looking around.

"Mom, what are you looking at?" Meghann moved in next to her.

"I think we need to fix up the kitchen. Your dad always meant to, but we never did it."

Meghann shifted a cautious look in Max's direction. "Max is going to do some work on the house, Mom. He'll update some things so they are safer."

Patricia nodded. "I do silly things sometimes. I probably could be safer."

"Yeah. That's what Ryan and I want for you."

"Who is Max?" Patricia asked, her back still turned toward him.

The sting of her words hit him right in the chest. "Mrs. Carr, I'm Max." Patricia turned to face him, unfazed that a man had spoken in her kitchen. "Max Devereaux."

Patricia smiled sweetly. "It's nice to meet you. Have I met you before?"

"Yes, ma'am, we've met."

"I'm so sorry. I forget things sometimes."

"I understand. I forget things sometimes too. Meghann, Ryan, and I have been friends for years. I brought you dinner. I think you were going to find some plates and we were going to eat on the patio."

Patricia nodded and a small smile formed on her lips. "Yes. Yes, that's what I was going to do."

As Patricia began to open cupboards, Meghann shot him a look that could only be described as sad. She was watching her mother slip away, and it broke Max's heart. He wondered how she could ever go back to New York as long as her mother was in this state.

Meghann moved in to help her mother gather plates as Ryan came through the front door. He carefully eyed the situation, and then the bag in Max's hand.

"You brought food?" he asked.

"I told your mom I'd bring dinner over. I knew she liked Frank's barbecue."

"She does."

Patricia turned her head toward her son. "Ryan, will you get that platter from the shelf up there? I think I have cookies in the pantry and we'll set them out for dessert."

Ryan retrieved the platter as she'd asked, but when Patricia opened the pantry, there were no cookies.

"I could have sworn I had some. I wonder if I ate them all and forgot to put more on my list. I'll bet your father ate them all. He sneaks snacks all the time."

Ryan and Meghann exchanged looks, but didn't call her out on her mistake.

They gathered the plates and made a pitcher of lemonade, then walked out to the patio to eat the dinner that Max had brought.

Before they began their meal, Patricia wanted to say grace. As Max closed his eyes and bowed his head, he felt Meghann take his hand and give it a gentle squeeze under the table.

CHAPTER 6

The barbecue was a hit, Max thought. Or maybe it was that while she ate, Patricia seemed to be in real time. She knew the day, and that Meghann was visiting from New York. She knew Max, and that he and Meghann had gone their separate ways when Meghann had moved to New York.

She understood that she was sick and was grateful that her children were doing things to make her comfortable. But all the while, sadness crept into her eyes.

"This has been lovely," she said taking Meghann and Ryan's hands. "I love you both so much. I'm glad you're here. And Max," she drew his attention to her, "I've missed you. You will always have a special place in my heart."

"Thank you, Mrs. Carr."

"Patricia. You can stop being so formal," she said and he nodded in agreement. "I'm going to head to bed. I'm worn out from today."

Meghann stood with her mother. "I'll help you."

"No. Right now I feel really good and I can make it." She kissed Meghann on the cheek, and then Ryan when he stood.

Max felt the need to stand as well, and Patricia motioned for him to come to her and she placed a kiss on his cheek as well before disappearing into the house.

The moment she was out of sight Meghann all but fell into her chair. Ryan eased back into his, and Max circled back around the table.

Meghann pressed her hand to her head. "That was one of the most exhausting days I've ever had," she said.

Ryan picked up his lemonade and took a sip. "One moment she's off the rails and the next moment she knows everything."

"This is common, isn't it?" Max asked. "Isn't that part of this disease? I read up on it a bit."

Ryan nodded. "The progression rates vary from person to person. For some it attacks fast and takes them. For others it could be years. At some point we'll have to put her in a facility."

Meghann shook her head. "I don't want to do that."

"And how are we going to keep this up? You're the one who said it was exhausting, and that's been one freaking day, sis."

The tears started immediately, and Max reached for her hand. "I can't come back for good. I'm buying time now, but…"

"She needs you as much as she needs me. Can't they play reruns of that stupid cooking show for a few months? That might be all she's got left, Meg."

Meghann let go of Max's hand as she picked up a napkin and wiped at her eyes. "I don't know what to do. If I stay longer I might lose everything I worked so hard for."

Ryan shook his head and picked up his plate. "I'm going home for the night. Call me if you need me. I'll be back early in the morning."

Max watched as Ryan disappeared into the house. Meghann sobbed, wiping away her tears as quickly as they fell.

"It's going to be okay," he said, and that caused her to lift her head and narrow her eyes.

"How? How is this going to be okay? My mother is slipping away from me, and I can't stay here to take care of her."

"I'm with Ryan. Why not?"

Meghann threw down the wet napkin and began to gather the plates. "I'm not having this conversation with you, Max."

"No one else is here," he said standing and picking up the remaining glasses and the bowl of potato salad.

He followed her into the house and set the items on the counter next to where she'd discarded the dishes she'd carried in.

"Walk me through it, Meg. Why can't you be here?"

"Go home. I don't have to have this conversation with you."

"I'm not going anywhere. You owe it to me."

"I don't owe you anything."

"You're the one that asked for my help. Not the other way around. If I don't completely understand the situation, how am I supposed to do the right thing?"

Meghann pressed her hands to the countertop. "Production starts next month. I'm supposed to be in planning meetings right now. I'm getting calls all day with questions and commitments that need to be rescheduled. It's a lot to take in. I don't know how much longer I can stay here."

The more she talked, the angrier he got. "I wasn't worth staying for, but I think your mom should be," he said as he walked out of the kitchen.

"Seriously?" she called after him and he turned to her as he put his hand on the knob of the front door. "Is there a time when you won't throw that in my face?"

"I think part of the problem was I didn't throw it in your face enough."

"That's low. We agreed, together, that it was an opportunity I had to take, and I'm damn glad I did."

"Fine. Then I guess it's your battle to figure out. Don't push any of this on your mom, Ryan, or me. I agree with him. You should be able to have some say if you go back or if you take some time. You've netted that company plenty of money just on your beautiful face and voice alone. They owe you now. You need to be here with your mom and me—Ryan," he corrected quickly. "I'll be back in the morning with the handrails for the bathroom. We'll start there."

Max opened the door and took the first step before she caught up to him.

"Don't leave mad, please," she begged and he stopped at the bottom step.

He turned when he heard her taking the steps toward him.

It was as if five years hadn't passed, and in that moment, Meghann moved to him, wrapping her arms around his neck, and Max, in turn, wrapped his arms around her waist.

She pressed her forehead to his. "Thank you. Thank you for being here. I needed you," she said as she pressed her lips to his.

Every emotion he'd ever had for her swirled in his head as she continued the kiss. There was no reason he should continue with her lips on his, but he couldn't help it. It sucked him in, body and soul.

Meghann leaned into him and deepened the kiss, and Max took it. His hands slid up her back and into her hair.

Which one of them would have the common sense to pull from the other?

It had to be him, and so he did—regretfully.

"I'll be back tomorrow," he said, nearly cold, as he turned from her and hurried to his truck. Without looking back, he drove away.

CHAPTER 7

The pity party Max was throwing for himself was epic. He'd driven straight home, opened a beer, and sat down on the couch. Meghann was going to leave again, he reminded himself. The internal struggle he'd seen within her proved to him that she couldn't stay with him, she had to finish what she was called to do.

Max pulled from his beer and aimed the remote control toward the TV, turning it on. This wasn't his battle to have. He was being hired to do a job, it didn't mean he needed to get involved.

And that, he knew, was just a lie he was telling himself to not feel the impending pain that Meghann's departure was going to cause.

When the channel switched to the next commercial, wouldn't it figure it was Meghann talking about *Dinner Dishes*.

Max clicked off the TV and just sat there. Perhaps he'd go to his brother-in-law's tap house and sit among the people. Wallowing in his self-pity was going to make him crazy.

. . .

OLIVER, a partner in the tap house, was pouring beers when he arrived and walked up to the bar.

"Hey, Max," Oliver said his name enthusiastically. "Did you come for the fish taco truck?"

"No, I indulged in barbecue from Frank's, earlier."

Oliver moaned. "That's my favorite on days I choose to eat meat."

"Isn't it everyone's? Hey give me that new stout you have on tap. When did that come in?"

Oliver reached for a glass and began to pour. "Spring selection. Just tapped it this weekend."

He pushed the glass toward Max who sipped it. "That's nice."

"It's easily a new favorite."

Max sat down at the bar. Oliver hadn't asked if he wanted to start a tab because they'd worked out an agreement that Max would do improvements at the tap house when needed, and he could always drink for free. But he was sure to tip well.

There were two different baseball games on the TVs throughout the bar. Max sat back on his stool to see them both as Oliver filled another glass. Again, Meghann's commercial aired, and Max drank down his beer.

"Did I hear correctly that she's a local girl?" Oliver asked.

"Yup."

"And I also heard you were going to marry her?"

"Yup," Max said as he pushed the empty glass toward Oliver, and he filled another.

"She's beautiful, man. What made you give that up?"

Max took the glass as Oliver pushed it toward him. "*Dinner Dishes*," he said referring to the show's title. "Sometimes dreams are bigger than relationships."

"Don't I know it," he said as he pulled another beer for the couple who had walked up to the bar. Then he returned to Max. "You guys didn't think about long distance?"

Max shrugged. "Long distance is one thing when you're

dating. It's another when you have a ring on her finger and a budding business to run."

"Tough breaks. Do you ever talk to her?"

Max sipped from the glass. "Not much. Couple of times in the past five years, but she happens to be in town at the moment."

"And that would explain you drinking in here on a Tuesday night. You usually wait until your family is here."

So, he'd noticed. "Just didn't want to sit in my house and have a pity party."

"Stay as long as you want," Oliver offered as he began washing glasses. "But if you're here at close you have to stay and clean."

CHASE WAS PULLING a limousine out of the garage the next morning when Max began to drive off the construction lot.

He noticed Chase was in his driver's uniform, and he pulled over and rolled down the window.

"Big boss man is driving today?" he shouted toward his brother as the sun began to illuminate the sky.

"Every Wednesday for years. When you have a paying client that likes your style, you give it to them. He tips good at Christmas, and by next Christmas little Kennedy is going to need some things from Santa."

The fact that Chase would now work the early hours just to save and buy his daughter, who would only be over a year by then, something awesome for Christmas, said he'd changed —a lot.

"Have a good drive."

"Hillary said Meg is in town," Chase said back and Max wished he'd have driven off.

"Yeah. Her mom has Alzheimer's and they asked me to do some work on the house to keep her safe."

"Oh, man, that sucks."

Max had only spent a few hours around her the day before and he could see how it would quickly wear a caregiver down. "She had a rough day yesterday. Mostly forgetting people and times."

"Big question is, did she remember you?"

Max smiled. "Most of the time. And when she did she thought Meg and I were still engaged. She's waiting for grandkids."

Chase clutched his chest. "That breaks my heart. Sincerely, man."

His too, Max thought. "I'm going to go inspect build sites and then head over to her house to install bathroom rails. I'll be over to your place after that to finish up your bathroom. We're within a few hours of completing it."

"You do what you have to do for Meg. We can wait. Is she going back to New York?"

"Can't imagine she wouldn't. She has a contract. Her life isn't here, and at some point I think they'll have to take their mom somewhere to get some assistance. I don't know how they'll do it alone."

"You okay with her around? I mean, wow, in town a day and she's already knocking on your door."

And kissing him. He processed the memory of the night before. "We're still friends. I'd do anything to help the family and she knows it."

"I'd better get going. I'll see you around. Are you going to be at trivia night Thursday?" Chase asked.

"We're champions. I can't let you try to stay on the leader board without me. Although, I did think Kennedy was smarter than she obviously is," he took the dig at their older sister.

Chase chuckled. "I might tell her you said that."

"She'd never believe you."

He waved as Chase walked back to the car that was running and waiting, and Max headed out into the world while the sun rose.

CHAPTER 8

M ax could hear the voices from inside the house when he knocked on the Carr's door. They didn't sound kind and welcoming, and anyone else would have headed back down the stairs and come back later. But something made him stand there until the door flung open.

"I can come another time," Max said as he looked into Meg's angry eyes.

"No, I need you. Right now," she said as she pushed open the door and then headed back down the hall. "C'mon."

Max set his bucket of tools and the rails he'd carried in with him down by the door, and followed her to the bathroom in the hallway where Patricia was sitting on the floor, half dressed.

He took a step back so that he wasn't looking at her and perhaps she couldn't see him either.

"Put a towel over your lap," Meghann said to her mother. "Max doesn't want to see you like this."

"Who is Max? Why do you have a boy here?"

That put an ache in his chest.

"He's here to put those railings up so you don't slide off the seat again. But he's going to have to help me get you off the floor."

"Fine," he heard Patricia say.

Meghann nodded her head for him to come toward her, and Max did. When Patricia looked up at him, she smiled. "Oh, Max! How nice of you to come by. I'm a little clumsy."

"Hello, Mrs. Carr. Let me help you get up off the floor."

Max stepped up to one side of her and Meghann to the other. Patricia Carr wasn't a big woman, but unable to use her own strength it took them both to get her back on the toilet seat so that she was stable.

Meghann was batting away tears as she turned her head. "I'm going to get your walker," she said.

"Like hell. I'm not using that damn thing."

Max wondered if he would help or harm the situation. But he decided, if she remembered him in that moment, maybe she'd listen.

"Walkers are amazing contraptions, aren't they? Seriously, when my dad uses his, he's three times faster than on his feet," he said and he saw Meghann's eyes go wide.

Patricia nodded. "Meg, get that walker. What are you waiting for?"

Meghann hurried off and came back with the walker. Max stepped out of the bathroom and into the hallway so Meghann could help get her mother dressed and out of the bathroom.

Meghann didn't say a word as they passed by him, but Patricia reached out and touched his arm.

When they'd cleared his sight, and gone through the kitchen and out to the patio, Max went for the rails he'd laid by the front door. It wouldn't take long to get the rails up, and then he'd head to his brother's house. He didn't think Meghann wanted him around much longer, or maybe he just didn't want to be part of the day she was having.

Within the hour, Max had rails anchored in the bathtub and

next to the toilet. He noted that the tub needed new slip resistant stickers. He also noted that the water heater should be checked, not only to make sure it was running well, but that the temperature was turned down, that way Patricia could never burn herself with the water from the faucets.

The flooring in the bathroom was tile, and in good shape, minus a few tiles that could be replaced. It was a basic design, so if they didn't have extra tiles stored somewhere, he could match the existing ones.

The light fixtures didn't have anything to do with the safety of Patricia, but he could install some more efficient ones. They had extras on the shelves back at the lot.

As he turned off the light, Meghann appeared at the door.

"Rails are up," he said.

She reached around the wall and turned on the light. "That should help. Thank you."

"I made a few notes of things that would help in here. How about her bedroom? Does she need anything there?"

"Maybe tomorrow we can look in there and you can tell me. Mom has testing. Ryan is going to take her."

"I want to help her. I saw what you went through yesterday, and it was sobering seeing her this morning on the floor."

"That was new," she admitted as she pushed her hair back over her shoulder. "What happened to your father?"

He narrowed his gaze on her. "My father?"

"You said he used a walker."

Max chuckled. "My father is fine and dandy, living in Florida with a new girlfriend. But, if I've learned anything, it's that the older people get, the more they want to be like the Joneses or keep up with them and do better. If she thought someone else her age embraced a walker, maybe she'd use one. It was a crap shoot. It could have gone the other way."

"It might tomorrow."

"Well, then we'll readjust our approach."

Meghann leaned against the doorjamb, and he could see the exhaustion in her eyes. "Where are you going now?"

"I'm finishing up some improvements on Chase and Hillary's house."

"That one still gets me."

"Me too." Max chewed on his bottom lip. "Are you with her all the time? I mean, do you get some time away?"

"Ryan and I agreed to share the burden. I felt as if I owed it to him. He's been here since this started."

"How long ago was that?"

Meghann crossed her arms in front of her. "There have been signs for a while. Maybe before Christmas. But we didn't think anything about them. It was a forgotten name or item. Then she'd repeat herself a lot. It's just progressively gotten worse. Now she can't even sit on a toilet without falling off."

"The rails will help, a little." Max leaned his hip on the sink. "I was just thinking that maybe you could use a break. We do a trivia night on Thursdays at Kennedy's husband's tap house, next door to her boutique. Maybe you could be on our team for the night. I know everyone would like to see you."

"I don't know."

He reached out for her hand. "Really, you need a few moments where you don't have to be on alert. Seven until nine. They have food trucks and some amazing craft beers on tap."

The corner of her mouth turned up into a smile. "Food trucks? That does sound like an epicurean adventure."

And only she would think of it that way. "I'll let you know, but it sounds like it would be fun."

"Good."

Meghann stepped back and Max slid past her, picking up his tool bucket and heading for the front door. "I figure if I do only a few quick things a day, nothing that takes more than an hour, she won't be triggered by my presence."

"I think she likes your presence."

"Yeah, but I've seen her turn on you. If she's getting worse, I'll be some strange guy in her house."

"I just don't see that happening. But I agree. That would be best."

Max pushed open the screen door and stood for a moment taking in the sight of her. Everything inside of him urged him to lean in and kiss her, but it would only hurt them, so he simply smiled.

"I'll see you in the morning."

CHAPTER 9

Ryan sat in the recliner, his eyes slowly closing before he'd force them wide again. Meghann sat with her mother at the card table staring at a jigsaw puzzle.

Her mother had been quiet since dinner, but she was attentive to the task of trying puzzle pieces until she found one that fit.

When Ryan opened his eyes again, Meghann caught his attention.

"Why don't you go home and get some sleep. You look exhausted," she said.

"Later," he said, and she knew it meant after their mother went to bed.

"Seriously, we're good here."

He studied her before rubbing his eyes. "Okay. Thanks."

Ryan stood and touched his mother's shoulder. She looked up at him and smiled. "Thanks for coming by," their mother said before searching for another puzzle piece.

"I'm going to walk Ryan to the door, Mom," Meghann said.

"Oh, Meg, you don't have to go. You live so far away."

It was moment to moment with her, but Meghann was

learning to breathe through it. "I'm staying with you, Mom. I'll be right back."

Her mother nodded as Meghann stood and followed Ryan to the door.

"Can you be here tomorrow night?" she asked, keeping her voice low.

"Sure. You got plans?"

Meghann shrugged. "Max invited me to trivia night at the tap house. I don't know if I'll—"

He reached for her. "Go. We both need time away, and I get to go to work."

"It's not a contest."

"Didn't say it was. I think you want to go. You want to spend some time with Max."

Meghann shook her head and then tucked a loose strand of hair behind her ear. "He's being helpful."

"He's never been anything but."

"I'm not looking at specifically spending time with *him*. It would be nice to catch up with everyone. Kennedy, Chase and Hillary, Paige."

Ryan grinned at her. "And Max."

Meghann bit down on her bottom lip. "Some normality while I'm back home would be nice. Can you be here?"

"I'll be here," he pulled her in for a hug. "Call me if you need anything."

"I will."

Meghann had been in a conference video chat when Max had been at the house that morning. He'd scraped off the old slip resistant stickers in the bottom of the bathtub and added new ones, as well as fixed those few loose tiles in the bathroom. He'd marked them with a tiny dot of tape so they could steer their mother clear of them for the day.

Ryan had talked to Max while he was there, and assured him that Meghann would be at the tap house that night. What was she supposed do to, but show up?

Meghann recognized the building, though she'd never been in it. It was a turn of the century post office that had once been converted into retail and office spaces. But as she walked up to the building with its warm glow of lights filtering out through open walls onto the street, and the noise of happy people inside, she knew it was very different now.

As she stepped in, she noticed a wall of old mailboxes, which looked original. She wondered if they had been tucked away somewhere or if Kennedy's husband had brought them in specifically for the tap house.

People lined the bar, and all of the tables were filled with people. Nearly each table had a small tablet in front of them, and the TVs around the bar flashed a countdown to the trivia contest that was about to take place.

Meghann walked to the end of the bar where the sign said *Order Here.* There was a tap house in New York that she and her co-workers frequented. She was familiar with how it worked, and rather enjoyed the atmosphere.

"What can I get ya?" the man behind the bar with his well-groomed, long beard asked.

"How about that chocolate coffee stout?"

"It's one of our favorites." He took a glass and began to pour her beer. "You look familiar. Have you been in here before?"

Meghann shook her head. "No. First time."

"But you're local?"

"Was."

He set the beer down in front of her. "Oh, no, I remember now. You're the gal with the cooking show."

Meghann pulled out her wallet. "Meghann Carr."

"Yup." The man held out his hand. "Oliver Westcott."

"It's nice to meet you."

"I will assume that you are playing with the Devereaux clan?"

A hand came to her shoulder. "She's my partner tonight," Max said. "Give me another one and Kennedy wants an iced tea."

Oliver nodded and went about pouring the drinks Max ordered.

"I'm glad you came," he said, standing close enough that their bodies touched.

"Ryan said I had to."

"Good." Oliver handed Max the drinks. "C'mon, they're waiting."

"I have to pay for my drink," she said, her wallet still in her hand.

Oliver shook his head. "You're family, and family doesn't pay. Enjoy yourself," he said and then turned to wash glasses.

Meghann thanked him and slid her wallet back in her purse.

Her stomach had fluttered with nerves all day, but when Max's family saw her, and emptied out of the booth to hug her, she decided nerves had no place here. Kennedy had a baby in her arms, and a mile wide grin. Chase held the baby girl Meghann had seen when she'd cornered Max outside Chase and Hillary's house two days ago.

Paige took her hand and pulled her down to sit next to her. "Thanks to you, I got booted to the other team," she teased.

"Oh, I don't have to…"

"You have to play," she said as she laughed, and leaned in close to Meghann. "He seems cool and collected, but he's so freaking happy to have you here he's going to bust."

Meghann watched as Max entered information on the tablet. If it weren't for her mother's condition, she figured she'd nearly bust in his presence too.

Over the past five years, when she did make it back home, she did all she could to steer clear of Max Devereaux. There hadn't been a day that her heart hadn't ached to be with him.

If only they'd had it out before she left. Maybe if they'd thrown things, or said mean things, it would have been easier. But they hadn't. They'd spent that last night wrapped in each other's arms on a mattress on the floor of her apartment. Then, he drove her to the airport and kissed her goodbye—and oh, what a kiss.

Meghann pressed her fingers to her lips thinking of the kiss she'd planted on him after dinner the other night. The pull he had on her was tremendous, and it was easy to slide right back in as if she were family, just as Oliver had said she was.

"Okay," Max turned to her with the tablet in his hand. "It's you, me, Chase, and Hillary. The questions come up on the TV, and we answer them here. The faster we answer the better, especially if we have the right one." He chuckled and looked up at her. "Are you okay?"

Meghann lowered her hand and wrapped it around her glass. "I'm good. I'm really good," she said taking it all in, and realizing just how much she had missed him and his family.

CHAPTER 10

Max usually called it quits after two beers, but he was deep into his fourth, and Paige had slid him a bottle of water. She always had his back.

Meghann had nursed the same beer all night. She'd managed to keep them on the leaderboard, too. Hillary was occupied with their daughter. Chase was on his phone with one of his drivers. Most of the last round had only been Max and Meghann, and they were still on top.

Over the past two hours they'd inched closer and closer, to look at the tablet. Now Max's arm was on the back of her chair, and she was close enough he could smell her hair.

This would be a night he'd always remember. That one time when five years had simply melted away. But the reality was, she had to go back.

Max picked up his bottle of water and sipped. He had to remember Meghann wasn't there for him, she was there for her mother. And she'd asked for his help where her mother was concerned.

"His eyes are closed," she said, pointing to the answer on the tablet.

"What? Who's eyes were closed?"

"Aren't you paying attention?" she asked, and he thought she had no idea just how much attention he was paying—but not to the game. "In all the pictures of Forrest Gump in the movie, his eyes are closed."

"Hit it."

Meghann got on the board first, and as others added their answers, theirs stayed on top. Eventually when the countdown clock finished, she'd had the right answer first, and they'd won trivia night.

"I told you," she joyously shouted and elbowed him as Chase high-fived her.

Oliver appeared at the table with a basket. "Pick one. All four of you get one."

Hillary put her hand in the basket first, pulled out an envelope, and opened it. "Perfect. Starbucks gift card. I could use this to get going in the mornings."

Chase wrapped his arm around his wife's shoulders. "Pick me one."

Hillary drew out another envelope and opened it. "Lottery tickets."

"Oh good. Let's see if we're millionaires," he joked as they sat down and began to scratch their tickets.

Meghann and Max both put their hands in the basket at the same time, each pulling out an envelope.

Max opened his first. "Dinner for two," he said.

Meghann tore open her envelope. "One night at the Fisher's cabin?"

Oliver nodded, nudging Max's shoulder. "The Fishers are regulars who have a cabin about an hour away. Tucked into the trees by Clear Creek in the canyon. It's breathtaking. Paige and I drove up there to check it out one day and hike."

The mention of her name had Paige inching into the conversation. "It's beautiful. You'll love it."

Meghann handed her envelope to Max. "You should probably take this. I don't suppose I'll use it."

He took the envelope and looked at the certificate inside. He wasn't sure he'd ever use it without her.

"Will you share my dinner with me?" he asked.

"Oh, I'd have to see about arranging that."

"I can ask Ryan," he teased, but he eased back when he saw the seriousness of the situation cloud her eyes.

"I'm sure it won't be a problem. I just have to get over the guilt I feel when I leave her."

Max moved his arm from the back of Meghann's chair to her shoulders. "You have to take care of you too. This was a few hours. Dinner would be a few hours. You can't help her if you're not taken care of too."

"Oh, and you're going to take care of me?" her voice cracked with the threat of the tears he could see welling in her eyes.

"I'd take care of you forever," he said, and he hadn't even had to think about it.

Meghann drew in a long, deep breath. "I should go home."

"Okay. I'll walk you out," Max offered.

He waited until Meghann had composed herself, and then watched as she hugged his family goodbye, including his new nieces. Then, with his hand on the low curve of her back, he walked out of the tap house with her and toward her car.

"I HAD A REALLY NICE NIGHT," she said as she fished her keys from her purse. "Thanks for the invite."

"I knew we'd win if you were with us."

"I got lucky." Meghann pressed the key fob and unlocked her doors. "Thank you for everything, Max." She opened the car door and stood facing him. "You're making this whole situation with Mom easier on me."

"I've done very little. I'll be there every day to do more to keep her safe. Tomorrow I'm going to tack down the carpet in the hallway. I saw a few places she could get a walker caught in it. It's the original carpet, Ryan said."

Meghann nodded. "They never did many improvements, and now they need to be done."

"I'll take care of them."

Meghann stood there silent for another moment. "Thanks again," she said and moved in to hug Max, because it was instinct.

Instinct was a funny thing though, because when his arms came around her for a hug, they both moved in for the kiss she found them tangled in. It wasn't just a goodbye peck on the cheek or lips, this was heated, and even more involved than the kiss they'd shared at her mother's front door.

Her fingers moved into his hair, and Max's hands slid over her bottom as he pressed himself against her, pushing her back against the car.

Five years of need was stirring in her, and she couldn't break away. There was a deep-seated desire to have Max kiss her and touch her. In five years, she hadn't been touched by another man. It was a sad state to be in, to be in her thirties in New York and have taken herself off the market when it came to relationships. But there had never been a man she wanted more than Max. And now, in the street, she had him. His hands skimming up her body and his mouth on hers. How many nights had she dreamed of this very thing?

It had to stop. She had to go back to New York and he had to stay in town. They were going to go through the same heartbreak they did when she'd moved away, but she couldn't help but let the kiss linger—smolder.

When they'd run out of breath, they eased back so their foreheads were pressed to each other's.

She wanted to ask him to come stay with her, but she couldn't. And she was damn sure the same battle to ask her to go home with him raged inside of Max.

Before she said anything that would turn into regret, she eased herself into her car, and pressed the button to start the engine.

Max lingered between her and the car door for another moment, then he shut the door and stepped back.

Meghann put the car in drive, and watched as Max stood there, growing small in the mirror as she drove away from him.

CHAPTER 11

It was after lunch when Max finally pulled up to the Carr house. He'd finalized Chase and Hillary's projects by ten o'clock that morning, but since then his phone had been ringing all morning with issues on two different job sites.

Another round of phone calls as he loaded supplies into his truck, and he'd managed to put everything right with his crews. Now he sat in front of Patricia Carr's house as his phone rang again.

"I have a leak in my bathroom," Paige hollered into the phone. "The bathroom floor is flooded, and it's going into the basement."

"Turn off the water. Seriously, I have to tell you that?"

"Jerk," she snapped back. "No you don't have to tell me that. I just got home and there is water in the bathroom. I turned off the water to my toilet, my sink, and then went downstairs and turned off the main line. Can you help me, please? This is a bit of a crisis, and I only have so many towels."

Max looked up at Patricia's house, realizing that just beyond the door Meghann expected him to arrive to fix the carpet, just as he'd told her he would. And then would they address what had happened between the night before? Or was he going to just walk in and expect to kiss her like that again?

"Max!" Paige shouted. "Are you still there? I need your help."

"Do you still have that wet/dry vac I gave you for Christmas?"

"Of course I do. I have it in my garage, in the box where such a thoughtful gift should be."

Max pressed his fingers to his eyes. "I'll go back to the lot and get a wet vac and some fans. You're going to want to make plans to sleep somewhere else tonight. Those fans are going to have to run all night long."

"I'll go get that thing out of the garage and get started on this. Just get here, please. And thank you. I love you. You're the best brother."

"Until you need a ride somewhere."

That made her laugh. "I'll see you soon, and can I stay at your house?"

Max looked back at Patricia's house and sighed. "Of course."

THE PIPE under Paige's bathroom sink had burst. Max told her she should be grateful it happened in the spring. At least they could keep the windows open to help dry out the house.

Water had been leaking long enough that it had seeped under the flooring and soaked the ceiling in the basement.

Max worked on pulling down the basement ceiling. The enormous fans rattled on the floor above him. It was deafening. His phone buzzed in his pocket, and he was going to throw it across the room if it was his site manager one more time, but the name on the caller ID made him stop what he was doing.

"Meg?"

"I thought you were coming over today to fix the carpet. Did I misunderstand that?"

"No. I—"

"I saw you pull up and drive away, Max. I know I had no right to kiss you again, but I hired you for a job and—"

"Meg, stop."

"I should have just had someone else do it. Listen, I understand if you don't want to be around me. I get it. It's just that I trusted you in the house with my mom, and—"

"Are you going to let me talk, or are you just going to keep scolding me?" He was yelling over the rattling of the fans above him.

"Yes, I'm sorry. What do you have to say?" Her tone was condescending now.

"When I pulled up to your house, I got a call from Paige that she had some flooding at her house. I'm here now pulling down the basement ceiling and ripping up flooring so we can get it dried out. It's been a hectic day and I forgot to call."

He stepped off the ladder and walked to a slightly quieter corner of the basement. "I have all intentions to come and tack down that carpet, and I should have called. But, Meg, don't you dare think that I'm avoiding you. God, don't think that at all," he sighed and ran his hand over his head, realizing he had chunks of drywall in his hair. "Those kisses, well, they're going to keep me going for a long time. I've missed them. I know what's coming at the end of all this. I guess I figure I'm more prepared this time."

She was silent for a long moment. When he took a breath to ask if she was still there she said, "I'm glad I didn't run you off. And I'm sorry I got mad first and didn't ask if something had happened. I'm all out of sorts."

"As you should be."

"They want me back to start shooting. Max, I can't leave her like this."

His heart was aching as he listened to her, wishing he was there to wrap her in his arms. "I know. Why don't I come over in a bit when I have Paige's house secure. I'll fix the carpet tomorrow, but I'd like to see you."

He heard her sniff back tears. "I know you're busy, but I'd really appreciate that. Ryan was supposed to sleep here tonight, but there was a vet emergency."

"Seems to be a day for emergencies. I'll be there in a little while. Can I bring anything?"

"She keeps mentioning ice cream."

Max chuckled. "I remember what she likes. I'll bring some."

"Thank you. See you soon."

Meghann disconnected the call before instinct took over and he said *I love you.*

He tucked the phone back into his pocket and looked up at the hole in Paige's ceiling. He'd finish tearing out the wet drywall and get a fan down there before he left. It wasn't a job he could hurry, but he wanted to get out of his sister's house as quickly as possible. At that moment Meghann needed him, and he realized he needed her too.

CHAPTER 12

P aige had wanted to order dinner, but Max just wanted to get to Meghann and spend some time with her. He craved it, and needed it now. The fall later was going to be hard, but it didn't seem to matter.

"I'll be fine. Maybe I'll stop by the tap house and see what truck they have out there tonight." Paige packed a bag to take to Max's. "I'll need a key."

"I gave you a key when I bought the place."

"And that was like ten years ago. I have a drawer full of miscellaneous keys in my kitchen, and I don't want to sort through them."

Max growled as he took his key off his ring. He had another one stored in his truck, one in desk drawer at the office, another in the garage, and even one in his shed. He could spare a key, he supposed.

He handed it to his sister. "The spare room is made up, you can sleep in there."

Paige laughed. "I suppose you're the only man on the planet that has an actual spare room, and it's set up for just that. Any other man would have an office, a gaming room, or a room to collect junk."

"What good is a spare room if you don't let relatives crash there?"

"You're a unique man, Max Devereaux. Will you be coming home tonight?" Her lips puckered as her cheeks pinked with the tease of what else he might do.

"I'm going to her mother's house to see her. I don't expect to stay. In fact, I don't expect to ever stay."

Paige's shoulders dropped. "Someone saw you kissing her last night. Are you ready for that?"

Max shook his head. "No. I've kissed her twice now in the past few days, and I'm too comfortable with her here. Now they want her to go back and start filming again. It's going to hurt all over again."

"It's a new age, dude. There are airplanes. You can FaceTime. You can send freaking old-fashioned mail. Why does it have to be all or nothing?"

Max ran his fingers over the whiskers on his face. "Because all of that is too hard. When you love someone you want them physically right there with you. She has her show, I have my business. I can't up and leave this and I can't ask her to up and leave her career either."

"You're both stupid and stubborn." Paige zipped up her bag and hiked it up onto her shoulder. "Funny that five years didn't take the shine off the two of you. In just days, you fell right in line again. Why wouldn't you want that forever?"

"Right now she's dealing with her mom. It's not good, Paige."

"No, it's not good. And luckily for Meghann, she's got a lot of support. You're going to be there for it all and you're going to take care of the house, and of her, but who's going to take care of you when it's over?"

"I'll be fine."

"Like last time? You got so drunk you passed out on multiple occasions, and that's not your style. You fired your best manager and had to crawl to him to beg him back to work. You fell off a freaking ladder, and—"

Max placed his hands on his sister's shoulders. "I get it. I know it's coming this time. I'll be prepared."

"Max, I don't want to see you go through that again."

"I appreciate it. But I can't help it. I'm all in until she's gone."

Paige pulled him in and wrapped her arms around him tightly. "I love you, big brother. I'm here for you."

And that he could count on, his family would see him through this.

ONCE PAIGE'S house was secure, and she was on the way to the tap house to have dinner, Max headed to the grocery store to get Patricia ice cream—mint chocolate chip. This time, he picked up a bouquet of flowers for Meghann.

Meghann was sitting on the front step when he pulled up in front of the house. She looked so small—childlike.

Max put the truck into park and climbed out with his bag from the grocery store.

Meghann stood and walked to him. Without a word, she wrapped her arms around his neck and he pulled her to him.

"You're okay?" he asked as he pressed a kiss to her hair.

"I feel so lost, Max. Thank you for coming. I'm sure you had other plans."

As she eased back, he looked her in the eye. "I'd never have other plans where you're concerned."

Her lips trembled as if she wanted to say something, but he knew they both would keep quiet about the fact that neither of them had been willing to make concessions for the other. Even now, it was all or nothing—nothing but the stolen moments they would have while she was there to care for her mother.

"I have ice cream," he said, handing her the bag. "And the flowers are for you."

He saw the tears well in her eyes when she batted them away. "That was very sweet."

"How is she doing tonight?"

Meghann looked back at the house. "She's calm. Right now she's inside putting together the puzzle we've been working on. She's asked for Ryan six times. My father three times. She remembers my name, but wanted to know if I had homework to finish."

"Chances are she's not going to remember me."

"Be prepared. I don't know what to expect."

"We'll make it though. Remember, I brought her favorite ice cream."

Meghann looked into the bag again. "Did you buy Magic Shell?"

"Seriously, it's like you don't know me at all," he joked.

"She loves that stuff, but it's so bad for her."

"At this point, doesn't she deserve some sinning?"

Meghann reached back and took his hand, interlacing their fingers as she walked into the house.

Paige was right. When she left again, it was going to hurt like hell.

CHAPTER 13

"Mom, we have a visitor," Meghann said cautiously as they stepped into the house.

Max stopped just short of walking into the living room. Her mother looked up and studied him, then looked at Meghann who smiled at her.

"Do you remember Max Devereaux?" Meghann asked and Max took a few steps further into the house.

Her mother stared at him a moment longer. "Of course I remember Max. He brought me roses the other day."

Max tucked his hands into his front pockets. "Yes, ma'am, I did."

"I hadn't seen you for years."

"Correct, five to be exact."

"You should visit more often."

"Yes, ma'am, I will."

Meghann smiled. "He brought you mint chocolate chip ice cream with Magic Shell for the top."

"I do like that hard stuff on my ice cream."

Max nodded. "I remembered. Would you mind if I sat down and worked on that puzzle with you?"

Her mother looked up at her, as if in need of reassurance, and Meghann nodded.

She patted the chair next to her. "Max, come sit. Meghann, will you make us up some ice cream? And don't be skimpy with that topping."

Max passed by Meghann and sat down by her mother.

Meghann stood in the doorway for a moment and watched them. This should have been what it was always like. Her heart was so full she was sure it might burst watching them sit together, her mother explaining their process to him, and Max listening intently.

Max looked up and caught her watching them. He winked, and she knew she'd tumbled right back into that place she'd been five years ago—in love.

Forcing herself to walk away, Meghann walked to the kitchen and set the bag on the counter. She pulled out the beautiful flowers and sniffed them. Max was always thoughtful about small gestures like flowers, candy, cards, and little gifts that said he was thinking about her—or anyone that meant something to him.

As she pulled down three bowls, she wondered what she'd missed out on over the past five years. Surely, he'd have sent her little things and visited, had they not absolutely called it off when she left. The decision had been mutual, but they knew they had to make it a solid cut. If they didn't, one of them would have given up their dream for the other, and neither of them thought that was fair.

It broke her heart to know how happy they had been, and yet they were the couple that hadn't worked out.

Meghann opened the drawer with the kitchen tools, and pulled out the ice cream scoop. She studied it. They'd had it in that drawer since she was a little girl. The release on the trigger hadn't worked since then, but her mother had never replaced it. Much like the kitchen being updated, her mother just hadn't seen the purpose.

Filling the bowls, she added an extra scoop to each of them, and giggled as she did so. Then she shook the Magic Shell and generously poured it over the top. It felt freeing to have just a few moments alone in the kitchen not worrying about her mother.

She jumped when the back door opened and Ryan walked in. He chuckled at her pressing her hand to her heart.

"Did you save the day, Dr. Carr?" she asked as she licked the ice cream from her fingers and then wiping away the small dot that had landed on her shirt.

Ryan ran the back of his hand over his eyes. "I wish I could. A dog was attacked by something. It looked like maybe a coyote, but his injuries were too much."

Meghann laid her hand on his arm. "I'm so sorry."

"It's part of the job, Meg. Kind of like you burning something in the oven."

"Mine isn't a life."

"Depends on who eats it," he joked through his exhaustion. "What are you making?"

"Max brought mom ice cream and Magic Shell."

"Mint chocolate chip and Magic Shell? Is he trying for kid of the year?"

"At this moment, he's winning. She seems to remember him most often. At least when it comes to people outside the family," she corrected.

"Meg, he was family. He was present during a happier time in her life."

"Mine too," she said softly. "Do you want some?"

"Of course. I'm going to clean up real fast then I'll be out." He kissed her on the top of the head as he passed, and she pulled down another bowl.

When she carried the tray of ice cream bowls out to the living room, she noticed how focused her mother was as she worried over a piece and Max worked to help her find the corresponding space. Usually they would work the puzzle and watch TV, but they'd agreed to keep the TV off in case one of Meghann's commercials came on. Last time it had put a lot of stress on her mother, knowing she'd be leaving.

"You're being very generous," Max said looking at the tray. "There's only three of us."

Meghann laughed. "Ryan just walked in and wanted some too."

Her mother lifted her eyes to meet hers. "Ryan?" she questioned and then nodded. "Ryan," she repeated as if she'd had to think about who he was, but then remembered.

Meghann handed her mother a bowl and a spoon. "I laid it on extra thick," she told her and she was sure she heard her mother giggle before she took a bite. Then she handed Max his bowl just as Ryan joined them.

"Hey, Mom. You're making a lot of progress on that puzzle."

She nodded as she took a bit of her ice cream and held it in her mouth a moment to let it melt. "Max is helping me."

Meghann looked up at Ryan trying to read his face. What was it about Max that brought her mother calm, she wondered? Then again, he brought calm to everyone.

CHAPTER 14

Ryan offered to get their mother ready for bed, and Max joined Meghann in the kitchen to wash the ice cream bowls.

As Meghann rinsed them off, she'd hand them to Max who stood at the ready with a towel.

"I can't believe they never had a dishwasher in this house," she laughed. "Well, aside from us."

"What, you don't like doing dishes?"

"Not back then. Now, it's therapeutic. Of course, it's easy too. I only ever have one plate, one cup, and a set of silverware to wash."

Max set the bowl on the table and took the next one. "Just one plate? Always?"

Meghann chewed on her bottom lip. "Always just one plate."

"I would have thought over time you'd…"

"Always just one plate, Max."

He set the next bowl on the counter and took another. "They want you back in New York soon?"

Meghann nodded as she handed him the last bowl and began to wash the spoons. "We've been having virtual meetings. Everything is planned for the next season. I just don't know where Mom will be in all of this."

"Can't you tell them to wait?"

"It doesn't work like that. These people budget for this kind of thing. They have sponsors and advertisers to think about."

"Well, they should think about the talent, who needs to be home with her mother."

He set the bowl down harder than perhaps he should have, and then picked it up to examine it.

Meghann rinsed the spoons and handed them to him before turning off the water.

"What if it all ended, Max? I've thought about that for years. What if my draw wasn't good enough anymore, and what if they couldn't get sponsors anymore? I mean now, I have a prime spot. The advertising money is huge. Reruns, and cookbooks, merchandise, and products. All I need is a talk show and I'm Rachael Ray," she laughed, but then reeled it back in. "Right now it's in its heyday, and here's my mom going through this; lucky to have seen me a handful of times in the past five years. And us…"

Meghann turned to him as he put the spoons on the counter and hung the towel over the edge of the sink.

"We gave up on us so I could do this."

Max took her hands in his. "We had to. If we had tried to have a long distance relationship we would have ended up hating each other. And I'll go through the pain of watching you drive away again, just to have this time with you."

She eased in and pressed her hands to his chest. "I never should have kissed you the other night," she said looking up into his dark eyes.

"If you hadn't, I would have," he confessed as he wrapped his arms around her waist.

"What are we going to do?"

"Paige reminded me that there is FaceTime, Skype, Zoom, and

good old fashioned mail to keep us in touch. You don't work all the time do you?"

She let out a laugh. "It feels like it. It's certainly not a nine to five."

"Then here we are again, right? My business and family are here. Your career is there."

"I have right now, Max. Will you let me be yours for while we're together?"

He lifted his hand to her cheek and caressed it. "I've only ever washed one plate too, Meg. Only one."

Her lips trembled. "We'll figure this out, right?"

"We'd be stupid not to try." Max dipped his head to take her mouth as she lifted her arms around his neck again and held on for dear life.

When Ryan cleared his throat, they eased apart and Meghann pressed her cheek to Max's chest.

"Sorry to interrupt, but Mom wants to see you," he said.

She stepped away from Max and left the room.

RYAN STOOD there and Max adjusted the towel against the sink again. He thought perhaps it was time for him to go, but Ryan walked toward a cabinet and pulled down a bottle of whiskey.

"Dad put this up there twenty years ago. He said to let it age. I think we did that. Let's take it out to the patio," he said pulling down two glasses and walking out the back door.

Max could hear Meghann talking down the hall, so he followed Ryan out into the dark where the crickets serenaded them.

He sat down in the chair next to Ryan who poured them each two fingers of whiskey, then sat the bottle between them on the table.

Ryan examined the glass in the light that cascaded out from the house window. "The one thing I know with all my heart is that my dad is waiting for my mom. It kills me to say that, but I know my time with her is shorter every day, and he's just waiting."

"There's some comfort in that," Max agreed.

"Yep. Just like you were here waiting for my sister."

Max swirled the liquid in his glass. "Some things you just don't get over."

"Nor should you ever." He turned toward Max, leaning his elbows on his knees, and holding his drink in both hands. "She's pined for you. And I know your family: I've talked to them. You've been pining for her."

"Pining?"

"Let me have my old-fashionedness," he joked. "What I'm saying is, you were the first one she thought of when she got here. And yeah, she candy-coated it with bullshit about you being able to fix the house. And you can fix the house, but I knew she missed you. I think she works so hard so she doesn't have to think about you."

Max wished that would help him. It had never seemed to matter much. Every turn he took or place he went, he thought of Meghann.

"I can't leave my business. She can't leave her show."

"I think there has to be a compromise. And hell, I'm a big brother telling some guy this about my sister. But you're more than some guy, Max. You're the one, and always have been."

He knew that. "She doesn't have long before she has to go back. She's been back a few days, and already here we are stealing kisses like teenagers."

"Because when something is real, it never really goes away. I envy you that." Ryan finally lifted his glass in Max's direction. "Here's to the two of you figuring it out."

Max lifted his glass in a toast and drank down the whiskey only to choke on it just as Ryan did the same.

"Well, shit!" Ryan coughed. "Dad was wrong. This stuff didn't age well at all."

Max coughed too. "Too bad you're not a paramedic. We might need something to fix that," he laughed and Ryan did too as they hurried back into the house to find something to wash down the taste of that whiskey.

CHAPTER 15

Meghann walked into the kitchen as her brother and Max burst through the back door and pulled the milk container from the fridge.

Ryan pulled down two glasses and filled them, each chugging back the milk.

"What are you two doing?" she asked, watching the antics unfold.

"Dad, lied. That whiskey didn't age well, it went rancid," Ryan finished his milk.

"And you drank it?"

He nodded. "Disgusting."

Ryan walked to the sink and rinsed out his glass, and then took Max's and did the same. As he turned, Meghann shot him a look that had him turning back to the sink and washing the two glasses properly.

"I should be going home," Max said, tucking his hands into the front pockets of his jeans. "Thanks for the drink."

Ryan chuckled. "We survived it. Now to fix the rest of what's wrong with the world," he teased.

Max took Meghann's hand and they walked to the front door.

"Thanks for coming with ice cream," she said as Max turned to her, placing his hands on her hips, and pulling her close to him.

She raised her arms and wrapped them around his neck. She could smell the alcohol and milk mixed on his breath.

His thumbs brushed back and forth against her sides where her shirt had risen up when she'd lifted her arms. It was so very intimate.

"Is it safe to assume we're good here until you leave? I mean, that we've fallen right back to where we were five years ago when you left?"

"Do you know how many times I've been back in five years and always considered calling you?"

"It would have confused things."

"That's why I didn't. We made our decision."

"But this doesn't help the decision we made back then." His hands came to her back, under her shirt. "We have to decide if we keep stealing kisses, where does that lead? If we keep moving forward, what happens when you go back?"

"I'm not ready to think about it."

"So next weekend, we could both be broken again?"

Meghann pressed her forehead to his. "Maybe."

"I'd go through it again, just to have you in my arms again."

Meghann eased back. "Ryan will have the weekend off. He promised me he'd take care of Mom all weekend."

"We could use the gift certificate for the cabin we won at trivia."

"I was thinking the same thing."

"Were we stupid to call it all off? I mean, we didn't even try to make it work long distance."

Meghann shook her head. "No. Because here we are, right where we left off, and I respect and care for you. If we'd tried to make it work, something would have fallen apart, and then we'd have hated each other."

"I've never watched one of your shows," he admitted.

Meghann let out a laugh. "Never?"

"Can't do it. Can't hear your voice and not want to run to New York and kiss you."

"Well, I'm here now. Kiss me now."

Max searched her eyes as he lifted a hand to her cheek, and then leaned in to take that kiss.

The warmth of his lips was intoxicating, and Meghann swayed against him, pressing her body to him, and causing him to stumble against the door. Their mouths still open to one another's as their arms maneuvered to hold the other closer.

Her head swam with all the possibilities of what could happen if she never went back. What would happen if she did go back and made demands for time with Max? Could they handle it now? They were older, wiser, and the heat between them hadn't fizzled out at all.

His tongue slid against hers and her knees grew weaker, until she was holding on to him for dear life.

Did she dare tell him she still loved him? Would it make it easier or harder to walk away? Why did it have to be so hard?

But she had to remember, she wasn't back home to make out with Max, though it had become a perk she didn't even know she was going to partake in, she was there for her mother.

The thought of her mission had her easing back, bracing her hands against Max's chest and fighting for air.

"I'm going to miss that when you're gone," Max panted out the words.

"Me too." Meghann stepped back. "I need to keep my head in the game. I have to remember I'm here for Mom."

Max quickly took her hand. "Don't go backing down on me because some guilt just stirred in you. You're taking care of your mom. You're doing a damn fine job. Both you and Ryan are. Don't forget to take care of Meghann too," he reminded her, running his hand down the length of her hair. "I'm not here to confuse things. But you called me to help you, and here I am. I'll help you with this house, and with your mother too. Take something for yourself, Meg. Let me fill that part where you need to feel special too."

He moved to her again, pulling her in. "We're adults. We can handle this."

Meghann rested her cheek to his chest. "She can't recover from this."

"I know."

"It's going to take her from me. I'm not even forty, and both of my parents will be gone."

His hand rubbed calming circles on her back. "You're not alone, Meg. Never alone."

She eased back and gazed up into his dark eyes. Placing a hand on each side of his face, she studied him.

"I want to tell you something."

"Anything."

"Don't hold it against me later."

Max let out a slow breath. "I promise."

"I love you, Max. I've never stopped loving you. And all of this confuses that."

Max took her wrists in his hands and pulled her hands from his face. His eyes had gone darker, and his face more serious.

"We're going to need counseling after this."

"It's not funny," she said, but realized he wasn't laughing, nor did he look humored.

"Meg, I've never stopped loving you either. I was serious when I said I only wash one plate. It's been a lonely five years, and what we did was the right thing. And now, you have your career. I have built my business. Most of all, your mother needs you—and me. We need to focus on that, day by day. But at the end of every one of those days, you can have peace in knowing that, Meg, I love you too. My arms are open to you. I don't know what's going to happen in the next two weeks, two months, or two years. Maybe we're that couple that has to wait it out until we're eighty," he said and she giggled. "No matter what happens down the road, know that I love you with all my heart, and I never stopped."

Meghann tucked her trembling lips between her teeth. "I want you to stay with me."

Max pulled her in close. "If your mother woke up and there was a man in the house, other than Ryan, it might go badly."

"I hate that you're right."

"Next weekend. You and me."

"It won't get here fast enough."

CHAPTER 16

The TV flickered in the living room and it took Max a moment to remember that his sister was inside, even though he'd parked next to her car in the driveway.

Honestly, he wasn't even sure how he'd gotten home. His mind had been blurred by the words *I love you.*

"You're later than I thought you'd be," Paige said as she muted the sound on the TV. "You doing okay?"

"Yeah. Actually, I am." He dropped his keys into the bowl by the door and fell onto the couch next to his sister. "She loves me."

"Ya. There isn't a person in this town that doesn't know that."

"She has to go back soon."

"And you're five years smarter. Are you just going to let her go this time?"

"I don't know what we'll do. I'd be willing to give up everything for her this time."

Paige turned to look at him. "That's pretty big. You have your own little empire here. I passed five projects with *Devereaux Construction* signs on them, just between my house and yours. The only reason you do piddly projects like modernize a house to keep someone's mother safe, fix my water damage, or build nurseries for Chase and Kennedy is because it gives you freedom to do the work you love and still manage your business—overseeing that everything is done the way that you want it done. I don't see you giving that up."

"I can't ask her to give up her life either."

"I don't think the two of you think straight. So," she inched closer to him, "what were you doing when she said she loved you?"

Max chuckled. "Making out at the front door."

"Oh, just like teenagers. Your truck doesn't have a back seat, would you like to borrow my car?" she teased as she nudged him.

"We won that night at the cabin during trivia at the tap house. We thought we'd go while Ryan is off work. She needs a few minutes away from her mother, for herself."

"For you."

"With me."

Paige moved in and kissed his cheek. "For the record," she said as she stood and handed him the remote, "I'll be here for you when you let her go and your heart is broken—again. That's what family is for."

He didn't have any words for that as she walked toward the spare bedroom and shut the door behind her.

Max sat on the couch a moment and then realized that Paige had been watching *Dinner Dishes*.

He unmuted the sound and listened to Meghann's voice. That was exactly why he hadn't watched the show, he thought. Sitting there, listening to her, had his body buzzing.

She still loved him. Max turned off the TV and rested his head back on the couch. There was no way in hell he was going to let her get away this time.

MEGHANN SAT STRAIGHT UP in bed when she heard the noises from downstairs. She pushed to her feet, taking a moment to find her balance when she realized it was the sound of the vacuum cleaner.

Rubbing the sleep from her eyes, she slid her feet into her slippers and headed downstairs.

Her mother was in the living room, lights on, TV on, vacuuming the carpet. She had her cleaning caddy on the coffee table.

Meghann looked at the clock on the wall in the dining room. It was one o'clock.

Not sure if she should say something to her, or step into her line of sight, Meghann assessed the situation from the bottom of the stairs.

When her mother turned off the vacuum, she looked up at her. "You need to get dressed. You're going to miss the bus."

"The bus?"

"Don't sass me," her mother said as she picked up a pillow from the sofa and fluffed it back into shape. "Ryan is already gone, and your father left early. You're the only one here, so you'd better get going. Make yourself some toast before you go."

"Mom, where am I supposed to go?"

"Meg, are you playing games with me? School. Now get."

Meghann took a few steps closer to the living room. "Mom, I'm thirty-five. I don't go to school anymore. I don't live here. Ryan doesn't live here. Daddy's gone."

Her mother took a breath to argue and then studied Meghann.

"You're thirty-five?" her voice shook as she asked the question.

"Yes. I live in New York, but I'm visiting you for a while."

"You live in New York," she repeated what Meghann had said. "Your daddy died before you left."

"Yes."

Her mother sat down on the sofa next to the pillow she'd just fluffed, and Meghann hurried to sit next to her. She was never sure which road she was supposed to take when her mother had episodes like that. Was she supposed to go along with it, or was she supposed to reel her back?

Her mother picked up the pillow, squeezed it, set it down, and then repeated the process one more time. "Max was here last night."

That made Meghann chuckle. "He was. He's been coming around."

"I see him once in a while, driving by the house or around town. He never stops to say hello."

"I broke his heart when I moved to New York. Remember, we called off our engagement?"

Her mother sat silently for a moment, her hands on her lap, twisting her fingers together. Then she nodded. "I forget things sometimes."

"Yes, you do. But I'm here for you."

She turned and studied Meghann. Her mother's lips trembled before smiling, but the smile didn't reach her eyes. "Thank you for coming here. I'm sorry I'm so much trouble."

"You're not trouble, Mama. You just forget things sometimes, just like you said."

"Ryan was here, too."

"We had ice cream and worked on your puzzle."

"With Magic Shell."

Meghann wrapped her arm around her mother's shoulder and pulled her in tightly. "You're right, Mama. With Magic Shell."

They both laughed and then it grew serious again. "I woke you with the vacuum."

"Yeah, because it's one in the morning."

"That's very early."

"I think so too," Meghann agreed. "Why don't we have some tea, and then go back to bed."

Her mother took her hands in hers. "I'm okay. I can just go back to bed. I'm sorry I forget things."

"It's okay, Mama." Meghann leaned in and kissed her cheek. "We can finish cleaning in the morning."

CHAPTER 17

Since Paige was already at an early morning yoga class, and had stayed at Max's house, he knew she wasn't going to be at her home. He headed straight over to her house the moment he got up to see how the drying was coming along.

It was going to take a few days to get all the water dried up enough to go in and fix the ceiling in the basement, the wall under her sink, and the flooring in the bathroom. So, he'd have a roommate for most of next week.

That wouldn't usually be a problem, only now he had a woman he'd like to bring home, and his sister was in the way.

He chuckled to himself as he cut away more drywall under the sink and carried it out to the trash. It wasn't as if Meghann was going to be able to get away and spend time with him at his house. Well, unless Ryan wasn't on call.

And, as if she knew he was thinking about her, his phone rang. "Hey, good morning," he said, walking toward the front door to get away from the noise of the fans that still whirred in the background.

"Breakfast. I need breakfast, and Ryan is here. Can you join me?"

Max looked down at his watch. He had a site to walk in a half hour. "Do you remember where the old newspaper building was located? West side of town?"

"The big building by the highway?"

"Yeah. They're turning it into studio apartments, but I have a walk through in a half hour. After that I can be all yours. And the area has changed a lot. There's new restaurants and bakeries."

"I'll meet you there."

"Hey, tell your brother thank you."

She giggled into the phone. "I'll do that. I'll see you soon."

She disconnected the call, and Max went back into the house to make sure everything was secure.

MEGHANN SLOWED as she pulled up in front of the old building with the large chain-link fence around it. It looked as if it had never been a warehouse, she thought.

The thick concrete walls now had windows and doors. It reminded her of the studio she filmed in in New York. It had once been an old warehouse that had been refurbished, and her studio kitchen was made to look like one right out of a fancy house.

Max's truck was parked in front of the main gate, next to three more trucks with his name on the side. *Devereaux Construction.* When Meghann looked around, she noticed the name was everywhere. From the banner on the side of the fence that announced who was doing the construction, to the big machines inside the fenced off area.

Max wasn't just updating kitchens anymore, he was changing the way the city looked.

Guilt washed through her when she thought of what he would have had to give up if she asked him to, five years ago. That was why they had decided on a clean break. She looked around at what he'd built and she nearly burst with pride. But there was loss there too. She couldn't ask him to give it up now either. Just as he'd never ask her to do the same.

Max stepped around the front of his truck and waved her over. She hadn't even seen him standing there.

Meghann stepped out of her car and joined Max and the men who had a set of blueprints rolled out on the hood of his truck. He introduced her to the others, and the conversation continued on about the plumbing in one of the units.

"Let's go look," one of the men wearing a *Devereaux Construction* shirt said.

"We'll be right behind you," Max told the men as he rolled up the prints, then opened the door to his truck and slid them behind his seat. Then, he pulled out two hard hats and handed her one. "C'mon, let's go see what they're talking about."

"You want me to go in there with you?"

"Yep. Come see what we do every day."

Meghann put on the hat, and he took her hand, interlaced their fingers, and led her thought the gate, shutting it behind them.

The site was mesmerizing to her. Meghann loved the feel of new, she decided. Some units were still open walls, but the one on the corner of the bottom floor was showroom ready.

"They're nearly fifty percent sold," he said softly to her as the men in front of them pointed out items that needed to be checked. "The whole project is slated to be finished by October."

"I still can't believe this is the same place that used to print newspapers. I also can't believe you have a construction company this big. Your name is on everything. Once upon a time it was you, your truck, and a trailer."

"Those were the days," Max chuckled. "Maybe one of these days we could drive around town and I'll show you what else we've built. I think you'll be surprised at what we can do with rundown areas."

He was beaming with pride, but that stab of guilt still twisted in Meghann's gut. This brief interlude of them falling right back into the relationship they had severed was going to hurt when she went back to her life.

Maybe she needed to invite him to New York to see what she'd built too. What would he think when he saw her studio apartment? Would he be impressed?

What would he think of the set she worked on, or the story-board layouts to one of her shows? Would he be as impressed by her as she was by him?

Yes, she thought again, inviting him out to New York was exactly what she would do. Then they could each see they'd done the right thing, or so she continued to try and convince herself as they toured the model studio, which was finished and staged to sell the rest of the units in the building.

CHAPTER 18

Walking away from the construction site, Max took off his hard hat, so Meghann followed suit, running her fingers through her hair, hoping it didn't look too bad. She handed the hat back to Max who opened the door to his truck and placed them in the passenger seat.

"Why don't we walk to breakfast?" he offered, closing the door, and taking her hand. "It's about a block without a sidewalk, but then you won't believe what they did to Cross Street."

"Cross Street. Wasn't that rundown? Lots of homeless camps?"

"That's what I'm saying. It's all upscale now."

They began to walk, their fingers interlaced as if they'd been doing it every day for the past five years.

"So what did they do with the people who lived here?" she asked.

"No one lived here. That was the problem."

"People were living here. Society just chose to not see them."

Max shifted a look in her direction. "And it's that heart of yours that I miss."

"It's humanity, Max."

"It is." He gave her hand a squeeze. "You'll be happy to know, that when the city took over this part they worked to do what was best for them. They took two years to focus on the people down here first. There is a new mission and outreach about two miles down the road. It has beds, meals, and medical care. Sure, some of them just relocated, but the city put in some work."

"I'm glad to hear that."

When they turned onto Cross Street, Meghann let out a noise that caused Max to chuckle.

"You're right. This is different," she said.

"I told you. We refurbished the second building on the left into condos, and storefronts on the street level." He pointed to the building with a bookstore and a coffee shop. "And in the next block, do you see that blue awning?" Meghann nodded. "That's a fine dining restaurant. White tablecloth kind."

"Who would have thought?"

"There's a little place just up on the right that's a breakfast place. They're only open until two. There might be a line, but it won't take long."

"So this is a hot spot, huh?"

"For sure."

As they walked past stores and restaurants that had once been abandoned buildings, Meghann thought about New York.

"Would you consider coming out to New York to see me?"

Max's pace slowed. "That sounds like an adventure."

"I want you to see where I live, and my studio. This has been fun seeing what you've been doing the past five years. And here I thought you were still remodeling kitchens."

Max chuckled. "I had to throw myself into more."

"I'm proud of you," she said, and this time he stopped walking.

"You're proud of me? What about you?" He turned to her. "I can't watch TV without your smile popping up. I can't go to Walmart without seeing your face on a box of pans, or on cookbooks. You've created an empire."

"I created an idea that someone bought."

"That's part of business, Meg."

"It kept my mind occupied and busy so I didn't run home."

Max stepped in and wrapped his arms around her waist. "You must pull some of those strings."

She thought about it. "I have some leverage. But I see what you're building. I know you understand V.C. and budgets. Investments and productivity. We're both the man behind the curtain at this point, aren't we? We're pulling all the levers, but we're not free to make our own lives happen."

Her heart was beating faster, and for the first time since she'd signed on to do *Dinner Dishes,* she sounded unhappy in her choice.

"That's bullshit," he called her out and she took a step back, out of his arms. "Five years ago, we thought we knew what we were doing. We were going in two different directions, and we knew if we didn't make a clean split of it, one of us would lose out on what we wanted. I'm big enough to say that hurt like a son-of-a-bitch for years. Now, I run the shots in my business, and make time to fix my sister's house, because I am pulling the levers. I know every single thing that goes on in my business, and I made it a well-oiled machine so I could do what I wanted to do. At this moment, I realize that I have a maximum of two weeks with you, pretending like five years didn't pass between the last time I held you and now. But, Meg, we're at the top of our game now. We do call the shots. Why can't we make all of this work for us? Isn't that what we've been working for?"

She hadn't seen the conversation circling the way it had. He was right. She didn't want to let go of whatever was building between them again. For five years she'd worried about what she'd missed out on—marriage and family with the man she loved.

An odd set of circumstances had given her a second chance,

and if she didn't pull some strings of her own, she'd lose him all over again.

"I love you, Max." The words flowed so naturally from her lips.

He pulled her to him again. "I love you too. I'm sorry. I get heated about this."

"I don't know what to expect. I love what I do, but being here, I can't help but miss this, too."

"I don't want either of us to give up what we've built. I'm willing to work through this. Meg, you have to admit that none of the feelings we had for each other have waned since we've been apart."

She laughed. "We're pathetic, aren't we?"

"Maybe. Or maybe we're just so in love that nothing can hinder it."

"I like that."

"Me too. Now," he released her and took her hand, "I'm starving. They have an eggs Benedict that is to die for."

CHAPTER 19

Max walked through the front door, and laughed at the music playing from his speakers. But he had to admit, it soothed him to hear the subtle tune of a flute and was that wind?

"Welcome home," Paige said looking up at him, her hair tied in a knot on her head, seated cross legged on the floor with her laptop in her lap. "I'll turn that down in a few minutes."

"You're just fine doing what you're doing. I'm only here for a moment." He studied her. "What are you doing?"

"Class planning."

For some reason, he thought when she taught yoga it just came from inside of her, just something she knew. He had no idea she planned it all out.

Max walked to the kitchen and pulled a bottle of water from the refrigerator as the music died down and Paige followed him, retrieving a water for herself.

"How was your morning?" she asked, leaning up against the counter and resting one of her feet on the inside of her thigh.

Max chuckled thinking he couldn't even lift his leg in such a way, and yet his sister stood like that.

"It was eventful. I was headed out to a site check and Meghann wanted to get breakfast. So we went down to Cross Street."

"You ate at that breakfast place, didn't you?"

"Best around."

"Yeah, I haven't brunched in a while. Maybe I should find someone to go with." She shifted legs, and tucked the other foot up against her thigh. "How is Meghann doing? I haven't seen her come back to class."

"She's stressed out and trying to be calm about it all."

"I should book her a massage at the wellness center."

Max sipped his water. "She could use it. You know, maybe you, Kennedy, and Hillary could take her to brunch, since you mentioned it. I think she could use some girl time."

"You always did take care of her," Paige said as she lowered her foot to the floor. "And on that subject, how are the two of you? You seem to have fallen back into what was."

He smiled wide. "It's like nothing changed, except we're older and in charge of our futures. We're going to go to that cabin, the one we won the gift certificate for, next weekend."

"You'll like it. It's beautiful."

Max leaned against the counter and crossed his arms in front of him. "Oliver said the two of you had been up there?"

"Oliver said we took a hike up there. Why does that seem to surprise you? I do work there from time to time. I know everyone who works there."

"Just didn't know you two were seeing each other."

"I didn't say we were. Are you making stuff up just because you have stars in your eyes? He takes my classes sometimes, and we decided to go for a hike one day. That's it. Friend. Nothing to dig for here."

"Anyway, we're going to spend the night together. I suppose that will make or break what we're toying with."

Paige shook her head. "Toying with. No one was ever more

suited for each other than you and Meghann. Most likely to marry and have kids. No one saw your split coming. Of course, I didn't see something like this coming either. Who would have thought you two would just fall back into sync?"

It was sync too, he thought—minus her mother's condition.

"I want to think that we could work it out. She could still work from New York and I could still carry on here, but I don't know."

"You love her. You'll figure something out," she passed by him and slapped him on the shoulder.

Yeah, he supposed they would figure something out.

MEGHANN CHOPPED UP VEGETABLES, water boiled on the stove, and the smell of a roast in the oven filled her senses. Oh, it felt good to actually be cooking in the kitchen again. There was nothing elegant about the meal she was preparing. A simple salad, a roast with potatoes, and buttered noodles. It was a carb overload, but a meal her mother would prepare for her father, and therefore a happy memory for Meghann.

Max would be joining them. Ryan was sitting on the back patio with their mother quietly enjoying the sounds of spring.

Meghann picked up the glass of wine she had poured and took a sip. She was grateful to have Ryan home for the night. There was a peace to knowing she could have a few moments of calm and a glass of wine.

The timer chimed, signaling that the roast was done. Before she pulled it from the oven to let it rest, she poured her noodles into the water.

When the back door opened, Ryan walked in and sniffed the air. "Oh, that brings back memories."

"I was just thinking that."

He picked up her glass of wine and sipped. "You're even drinking her wine," he teased.

"Can't cook this meal and not have a glass of wine, right?"

They both shared a laugh. "What is she doing out there?" Meghann asked.

Ryan sat the glass down on the counter. "I thought she was in here working on the puzzle."

A lump formed in Meghann's throat. "You were sitting on the porch with her."

"Yeah, with my eyes closed listening to the wind blow like you told us to do. She mumbled something about looking for a piece —I didn't think to ask to what."

"Ryan, she's not in here."

He hurried into the other room, and Meghann turned the burner off on the stove. She followed him, but their mother wasn't sitting in the living room.

"I'll check upstairs. You check her room and the bathroom."

They went their separate ways, but Meghann didn't find her in the bedroom, or the bathroom. She'd even checked the closet and under the bed, but she was nowhere.

Ryan made a thunderous noise as he ran down the stairs. "She's not up there anywhere."

Simultaneously, they ran to the back door and out into the yard. She wasn't on the porch or with her roses.

"Oh, shit!" Ryan yelled as he started for the gate on the side of the house that was wide open.

Meghann's chest hurt as she ran after him. The gate was one of the items on the list of things for Max to fix, and they just hadn't gotten to it yet.

Ryan yelled for their mother as he stood on the sidewalk. "You go down the street. I'll go up. You circle the next block and I'll circle this one. If we don't find her when we meet up here, we call the police."

She nodded, and started down the street.

CHAPTER 20

Max turned at the stop light and headed toward the Carr house. Meghann was cooking, and it had been a long time since he'd had one of her meals.

A woman caught his eye as she stepped off the sidewalk and a car zipped around her to avoid her. He shook his head. People just didn't pay attention anymore. But as he passed, he looked at the woman again. That was Patricia Carr.

Max pulled his truck to the side of the road and hurried out, waving down oncoming traffic to slow and go around them as he approached her.

"Mrs. Carr," he called out to her as he neared her. "Mrs. Carr, it's Max Devereaux."

Her eyes lifted to his and she reached for him.

He took her hands and guided her back to the sidewalk. "Mrs. Carr, are you okay? Where are you going?"

Her hands trembled in his. "I was going to the front yard to check the mail in the box."

"Okay." He looked around for her walker, but she didn't have it with her. Instead, he guided her toward the closest house and eased her down on the front step. "Let's take a moment and sit, shall we?"

"My husband will be home soon, and I need to start dinner. But this isn't my street."

"Can I give you a ride home?"

"Oh, no. My husband wouldn't appreciate that. He will drive by in a moment. He'll see me."

Now what was he supposed to do?

At that moment his phone buzzed in his pocket and Meghann's face appeared on his screen. "Hey," he said calmly.

"She's missing. Mom is missing," Meghann frantically yelled into the phone. "She's—"

"Hey, yeah, I'm here with her," he kept his voice soft. "Your mom went for a walk. She's about four blocks south of the house."

"Max! You have her? Oh, God."

He hoped Patricia couldn't hear Meghann's panic. "Bring your car, we'll wait for you. It'll be nice to see you again."

The line had gone quiet. He tucked his phone back into his pocket and turned toward Patricia.

"That was Meghann. She's going to come pick you up."

Patricia nodded. "That's very sweet of her. You know my daughter?"

That caused his heart to ache. The past few days she'd remembered him, but now he was just some stranger on the street.

"Yes. I know both of your children. They love you very much," he felt the need to say.

"They're good kids. My husband will be home soon," she repeated.

They sat and watched the cars go up and down the street.

A few minutes later Meghann pulled up in front of them and stopped.

Max stood and met her at the edge of the walk. He touched her arm and made sure she was looking in his eyes. "She went out to get the mail from the box. Her husband is on his way home, so we've just been sitting down."

He stressed his words with his eyes focused on hers.

"Max," she let his name out on a worried sigh.

"She's safe, Meg. Let's get her home."

Meghann moved around him and walked toward her mother. "Mom, let's get you home."

"Meghann, how nice of you to come. You've been gone for such a long time."

"Right. I'm here now. Let's go."

"Your father is on his way home. We should make him roast. He likes buttered noodles with his roast."

Max could see the tears streaming down Meghann's cheeks. "I know. That's Daddy's favorite."

He moved to them as Meghann began to help Patricia up. Taking her other hand, he helped them to Meghann's car.

Once she was securely inside, Meghann fell into his arms. "Hey, be strong for a few more minutes," he said pressing a kiss to the top of her head. "She needs you now more than ever."

"I'm not sure I can do this."

"You can. You're the one pulling the levers, remember? I'll be right behind you."

When Meghann had climbed into the car and started toward the house, Max hurried back to his truck and followed them.

Ryan was standing on the sidewalk waiting for them.

Meghann pulled into the driveway and Max parked on the street. He watched as Ryan hurried to the passenger door and helped his mother out of the car. With the skilled patience of a caretaker, he helped her up the front steps and into the house.

Max moved to Meghann's door and opened it. She sat there sobbing.

He knelt down next to her. "Let it out, baby. It's okay."

"It's not okay. This isn't okay," she shouted, still belted into her seat. "This isn't normal. This isn't safe."

He'd let her have her moment of anger, she was due.

"Ryan and I can't keep doing this, and at the same time, I don't want to lock her in some home where she's not with us or around her own things. I'm scared to death and I don't know what to do."

Max wasn't sure what he could say, so he remained quiet and watched as she frantically brushed away tears.

"I just want her to be okay. I want my mother back," she sucked in a breath. "I want to know that when I go back to New York and call her, she'll know who I am."

Meghann unbuckled her seatbelt and swung her legs out of the car. Max stood and took a step back. He'd hoped she'd fall right into his waiting arms, but instead, she climbed from the car and slammed the door, then paced in the driveway.

"What are we going to do? If I don't want her to go to some facility, then I'm going to have to quit. I'm going to have to give up my show, and quit writing my cookbooks. I'll have to move back here and give up my life in New York."

He wanted to ask her what would be so bad about that, but he knew this had nothing to do with him. At this moment she was spewing words and feelings, and he had to keep himself in check or his heart was going to break again.

Meghann wiped at her eyes again. "We should have fixed that fence first."

"I'll do it right now."

"What good is it now?" She threw her hands up in the air. "We might as well put a damn leash on her."

"Why don't we take a drive, or a walk, or something. You could use some air," Max offered, but when Meghann turned and her eyes had narrowed, he knew that hadn't been the answer she was looking for.

"You don't get it, do you? We can't leave her. Even with both of us here she got away from us. Our lives are over as we know it, and it's all about her right now. I don't have time for work, walks, drives, or meals away. I don't have time for you."

And that was when he knew he needed to leave before he said something. It wouldn't take much to jeopardize the past few days. If she could see past the anger she was currently feeling, she'd understand he wasn't against her—no one was.

When she'd fallen silent and the tears had dried, Max turned toward his truck to leave.

"Don't you have anything to say?" she called after him and he stopped as he reached for the door handle.

"I love you, Meg. That's all I have to say."

CHAPTER 21

Max drove through town—just drove. He didn't have anywhere in mind to land, but he needed to clear his head.

There hadn't been one angry word that Meghann had said that he took to heart, not against him anyway. He'd done enough work on himself over the years to know when someone was saying something hateful to him, or just clearing their mind of anger in his direction.

His mother had been infamous for sharing her opinion loudly, mostly about Max's father.

His father had had an affair when Kennedy was born. The woman had gotten pregnant, and Chase was born. Max's mother took his father back after that, and Max had been born, but shortly after that they'd gotten divorced. His mother had remarried, and was happy, even now, but she could hold a grudge, and everyone knew about it.

There were times when Max felt as if he'd only been a bargaining chip, leverage his mother used to keep his father. But his deceit had been too deep, and Max's mother just couldn't continue being married to him.

Max and his siblings gave their father credit where credit was due. He'd made a mess of things. He'd wrecked his marriage, and Chase's mom ended up divorced from her husband, too. But Carl Devereaux took his children seriously.

They all carried his last name, and therefore, were raised as a family. The three of them had different moms and different family dynamics, but his father kept them together as much as possible. When Max's father had married Paige's mother, and they'd had her, he included them in that family too. The four of them had always been inseparable, and they still were.

Recently, Paige had his back, and he had hers. Maybe next week he and Chase would pal around, or he'd have dinner at Kennedy's. He might have always felt like his mother's bargaining chip, but he was truly loved and accepted by his siblings.

But through it all, it had given him a thick skin. Thick enough that he knew Meghann was angry, and she had every right to be. Had he stood there and argued with her, her anger would have turned on him, and that would have confused things more.

In the morning, she'd have a clear head. When she was ready, she'd come to him. They would talk it out, and then they could decide the next step.

For now he drove down side streets leading to nowhere, just to give him time to think.

Eventually Max pulled up in front of the tap house. There was a bistro truck parked outside, and he thought that sounded interesting for dinner, especially since he didn't get to eat whatever Meghann was cooking.

He parked his truck, placed his order, and walked into the tap house through the side door. His sister sat at the corner table where the family would often gather, her daughter perched on her lap.

"Hey, stranger," Kennedy said smiling up at him when she saw him. "I didn't expect to see you tonight."

"I just drove by and thought I should get something for dinner. Wasn't much in the mood to cook for myself."

"You can join us. Joel was working, so we decided to come and be near him."

His niece raised her arms toward him, and Max pulled her from her mother's lap. "I'm going to get a beer," he said kissing Mati on the top of the head. "Are you going to walk with me?"

Max walked toward the bar with Mati in his arm. Joel smiled wide when he saw his daughter now reach for him.

"I'm afraid she's going to want to pour beer in her playhouse when she's older. What kind of trouble is that going to get me into when kids come over to play?" Joel humored as he kissed Mati's cheek.

"You'd better teach her to collect a cover charge."

That warranted a laugh. "What can I get you?"

"IPA, whatever is new."

One handed, Joel reached for a glass and filled it from the tap. "Alone tonight?"

"Yeah. Meghann's mom had a little issue, and it looked like it was going to become a big issue between us. So I left her to figure it out."

Joel slid the glass toward Max. "So you guys haven't seen each other in five years, she comes back to town and you're already back together?"

"There was an immediate rhythm. But I know she'll go back, and I'll stay here. Expect me to be in here, drinking more after that."

"I'll know to watch for you. Do you think there's a chance to salvage a relationship?"

Max shrugged. "I just don't know. She's extremely stressed right now. The fact that she asked for my help says I was still always present in her mind, right?"

"That's what Kennedy says. She says Meghann was your one and only."

"That's true."

"I hope it works out, man."

"I do too." Max reached his arms out for his niece again. "C'mon, let's let Daddy get to work."

Joel kissed Mati one more time and handed her to Max. He picked up his beer and carried it and his niece back to the table with Kennedy.

"You look natural like that. Beer in one hand, baby in the other."

"Can you imagine if things had gone the way I planned? I'd have been done with kids before you started."

"And you think about that, don't you?"

"Can't help it."

"How is Meghann's mom?"

Max sat down and situated Mati on his knee, pulling her toys across the table so they were in her reach. "Not good. Tonight she walked out of the yard. I found her walking four blocks away."

"That's terrifying."

"They're going to have to make some serious decisions soon on her care. And I just figured I was in the way."

"Is that why you're here?"

Max nodded. "Just giving Meg some space to breathe." Mati handed him a toy and he took it from her only to hand it right back. "Besides, I needed to be with my other girls for the night I guess. This is good for my heart."

CHAPTER 22

Meghann sat alone in the kitchen. The roast was dry and the noodles were mush in the pot.

Ryan had calmly taken their mother into her bedroom, talked her through what had happened, and caught her up to the timeframe of their life. At that point she'd decided she was exhausted, and he'd put her to bed.

He'd taken a phone call on the front porch, and Meghann felt his hand on her shoulder when he walked back through the door.

"I called in some favors, so I am free and clear for the next two weeks to be here." He pulled out a chair across from her and sat down, resting his clasped hands on the table. "We're going to have to decide what we're going to do."

"She could have gotten killed."

"Yep, and she knows that. Once she realized what year it was. But, Meg, it's going to get worse. There is no getting better."

"I don't feel right sending her to live somewhere that isn't here."

"Okay, then we have to consider in-home care."

"She's not going to want someone in her house that she doesn't know."

Ryan fisted his hands and released them. "Unless you're going to give up everything in New York to be with her twenty-four seven, we have to get help." His voice was rising in pitch and volume.

"I can't do that."

"I can't either. I just turned over my entire practice to other people so I could completely focus on this.. You left New York for the same reason, but they're already calling you back, right?"

"Yes."

"And what about Max? You came here and went right back into a relationship you had given up years ago. What happens now? There is a lot of shit to sort out here, Meg."

Her lips began to tremble and she pressed her fingers to them. "I hate to see her suffer like this."

"I do too."

"It breaks my heart to take her away from her house."

"I get it."

The first tear fell and Meghann wiped it away. "I love Max."

Her brother sat back in his chair and smiled wide. "I know that too."

"What am I going to do? What are we going to do?"

Ryan reached his hands across the table and took hers. "Let's go tour some facilities. Some of them are really nice, and they specialize in this. They'll take care of her, and she'll be surrounded by people going through it too. Meg, at some point she's going to turn on the oven or stove and burn the house down. Or decide she needs a bath and fall. She needs more than we can give her."

Meghann nodded, letting the tears flow freely. "You're right."

"And, I'm going to stay here, at the house until we get her settled somewhere. So you go pack a bag, and go find Max."

Meghann lifted her eyes to meet his. "Really? All of this and you're sending me away to spend the night with some man?"

"He's not just some man, Meg. He's the only man you've ever

loved, and I know you haven't dated since then. You don't even know what else is out there because you only ever loved him. So, go. Let him set your world right for a night. We've got a long, hard week ahead of us."

Meghann stood, and Ryan followed. She wrapped her arms around him and squeezed him tightly. "I love you. I can't imagine going through this without you."

"If there are any blessings to come out of this, it's that we were raised to be a tight knit group, and we are. And in the end, we will have each other, and she will be with Dad."

MEGHANN TOOK her brother's advice and packed a bag. She didn't want to call Max and tell him her plans. What if he didn't want to see her?

But surely he wouldn't turn her away if she just showed up.

His truck wasn't parked in the driveway when she pulled up in front of his house, but the TV flickered from the living room and there were lights on. She considered the fact that she hadn't been around in a long time. Maybe that truck was in the garage. Or maybe he left it at the lot and drove another car. He did have a motorcycle once, though she was sure he'd long ago sold that.

With her stomach twisted in knots, she climbed from her car and walked up the front walk. Her hand shaking, she pressed the doorbell and waited.

A woman's voice inside the house said, "One moment. I'll be right there."

Meghann swallowed hard. Maybe he didn't live there anymore, or worse, maybe he lived with some woman and had just been letting Meghann kiss him to make her feel better.

She turned to hurry down the stairs as the door opened to her back. She didn't turn around.

"Meghann, is that you?" the voice at the door called after her and that caused her to stop.

When she turned, she saw Paige standing in the doorway, a pair of yoga pants and a tank top on, in her bare feet.

"Oh, I thought maybe he had moved and it was someone else's house," Meghann laughed, not letting her know she was afraid he might be involved with someone.

"I'm staying here while he's working on my house. I had a pipe burst."

Meghann nodded, remembering that now. "Is Max here?"

Paige shook her head. "I haven't seen him or heard from him. Did you call him?"

"No. I didn't want to do that. Ryan stayed with our mom, so I just was going to show up."

"He's either at his office, my house, or at the tap house, depending on what food truck is there." Paige pulled out her phone. "Let me check their Facebook page to see which truck is — never mind. He's there."

She turned the phone around and showed her a photo that Joel had posted of Max and Mati sitting with Kennedy, with the caption *A family place.*

With her emotions still raw from her conversation with her brother, Meghann could feel the tears threaten. And seeing Max holding his niece gave her chills.

"I guess I'll head over there, then. Don't tell him I'm coming."

"I won't. Have a nice night," Paige said as Meghann started back down the walk.

As she climbed into her car and started the engine, Meghann thought about the picture Paige had shown her. Max didn't look mad, but had he sought out his family for support too? They did have that in common.

CHAPTER 23

Pushing away the container his food had been delivered in, and then moving it again to keep Mati's hands out of it, Max contemplated heading home. Though, he was more than grateful that his sister and niece had been there to keep him company.

"How long are you staying here?" he asked Kennedy as Mati rested her head on her mother's shoulder.

"Not much longer. Joel will close tonight, but I think she's had enough." Kennedy kissed the top of her daughter's head.

"I'll walk you out," he said as he picked up his box and Kennedy shook her head.

"You should stay."

When Max turned, he saw Meghann walk through the door and look around. Then she caught his eye and smiled.

Max stood and met her as she walked toward him. "Hey," he said softly. "I didn't expect to see you."

"I know. I wanted to apologize for my behavior. It was uncalled for."

"It's justified, and I'm a big enough man to know it wasn't

aimed directly at me, or at least not all of it. Is Ryan with your mom?"

"Yeah, he sent me."

Max owed him a thank you.

Kennedy appeared next to him with Mati now asleep on her shoulder, the diaper bag hanging from her arm.

"We're headed out, but I wanted to say hello. This one has had a full night."

"Hopefully I can catch up with you soon. I'll have to stop in your store before I go back to New York."

Max gave a glance to her wrist and noticed that she still wore the bracelet he'd had Kennedy make her so many years ago.

"I'd like that," Kennedy said as Joel walked toward her. "I'll see you both later."

They watched as Joel took the diaper bag and slipped his arm around Kennedy's waist and the family disappeared out the back door.

"Who watches the baby when she goes to work?" Meghann asked.

"I built a nursery at the store for her and Hillary. The girls are only hours apart."

Her eyes went wide when she looked back up at him. "Really?"

"Yeah. Hillary's baby came super early and Kennedy's was late. But they always did everything together, they might as well have babies together too." He leaned in and kissed her cheek. "I'm glad you're here. Did you eat?"

Meghann shook her head. "No. It was dry and maybe I just wasn't interested."

"C'mon. Let's get you something to eat and a beer. Do you need to hurry home?"

She shook her head. "No, actually, Ryan told me to pack a bag and go find you. I didn't realize that Paige was staying with you though."

Max let out a long breath. "You were coming to stay with

me?" She nodded. "Then Paige can handle calling on another sibling for the night."

MEGHANN WASN'T sure when he'd texted or called Paige, but when she followed him to his house, and parked in his driveway next to him, the house was dark and she knew Paige wasn't there.

As she put her car in park and turned off the engine, she took a moment to close her eyes and take in a few deep breaths.

If she walked into his house with him, she knew she wouldn't leave until morning. Kisses were one thing, words were another, knowing she'd sleep in his arms all night, with or without making love to him, was an entirely different thing. They'd already planned a weekend away at the cabin, but this was spontaneous.

When she opened her eyes, he was standing at her door. He stepped back as she opened the door and climbed out of the car.

"Are you having second thoughts?" he asked as she pulled her bag out from the passenger seat.

"No. Not second thoughts. Just thoughts."

"You don't have to stay."

"I want to."

"We don't have to—"

"Max," she lifted her hand to his chest, "I want to."

A smile tugged at the corner of his mouth. "I owe your brother big time for this."

"So do I. I wasn't handling it very well." Meghann looked at the house. "Where did you send Paige off to?"

"I don't have any idea. I texted her and told her you were staying the night and she replied with an all caps *I'M OUTTA HERE*," he said taking the bag from Meghann and closing her car door.

Then he took her hand and they walked to the front door.

As Max put his key in the lock, Meghann took yet another long breath. It had been five years since she'd stepped into that house. Back then it wasn't much to look at. There was no carpet or tile on any of the floors, and the cabinets in the kitchen had no doors. He'd started his remodel in the bedroom and was working his way toward the front door. Comfort for the time he was there was priority, he'd always say.

Max pushed open the door and stepped inside, turning on a light. When Meghann stepped in she took a moment to take in the sight.

Beautiful hardwood floors welcomed her. The entry opened to the living room with a large plush throw rug under a coffee table, in front of a comfy looking couch with lots of pillows. A large screen TV hung on the wall. The only photos on the end tables were of his siblings and his nieces.

The room opened to the kitchen, and her eyes went wide. "Oh, wow," she said as she moved toward the stove with the built in flat top and the stainless hood. The tiled backsplash and the farm sink nearly made her swoon. The subzero refrigerator begged her to open it.

"You have all this room and it's empty?" She turned to him and he eased a hip against the counter.

"I'm not here much."

"Can you imagine what you could cook in here?"

"Can you?" his voice had gone serious and his eyes dark.

Meghann swallowed hard, and shut the door. Without an answer, she moved on, and continued her tour.

The bathroom in the hallway was prettier than any upscale hotel, she thought. The door to the right was a guest bedroom. It was obvious that someone had slept in the bed and quickly pulled the sheets up.

Max reached for her hand and led her to the next room. He pushed open the door and stepped back.

The room was exactly as she'd remembered it, because she'd picked out all of the furniture and the bedding.

"You kept your room the same?" she asked as she walked in and he turned on the light.

"I liked it the way it was."

Meghann ran her hand over the wood grain on the top of the dresser, and reached for the post on the bed. The master bathroom caught her eye, and she turned on the light. He'd upgraded the fixtures and the tiles in there, and now there was a jetted tub.

"This is beautiful."

"It was therapeutic. I threw myself into finishing the house and building my business."

"You did an amazing job."

"Thank you." He set her bag on the bed and moved to her. "I'm glad you're here again."

Max put his hand on her hip and she leaned into him, her hands resting on his shoulders.

"I never thought I would be."

His arms wrapped around her and his hands pressed into the small of her back. "Why did you really come for me the other day?"

Meghann brushed her hands over the fabric on his shirt. "We needed your help, and I couldn't be in town and not see you."

"Is this what you were expecting?"

"Hoping—never expecting."

Max reached his hand into her hair and locked eyes with her. "Tonight the rule is we won't talk about what happens beyond today. I just want to be with you."

"Okay," she let her hands slide to the hem of his shirt. Tucking her hands under the fabric, she felt the warmth of his skin on her fingertips. "I came for you because I still love you, Max."

"Thank goodness," he said as he dipped his head and took her mouth with his.

CHAPTER 24

She was standing in his room, and Max couldn't help but to take what she offered. Meghann's hands were on his skin, her lips on his lips, and her body was in his hands.

Meghann pulled his T-shirt up and over his head, dropping it to the floor without a moment of hesitation between kisses. Her hands skimmed over his chest as he began to unbutton her shirt while his kisses trailed from her lips, down her delicate neck, and over her collarbone.

The sharp breath she took, and the bumps that formed on her skin, said that his touches and kisses were affecting her, and there was no doubt what they were doing to him.

Max spun her toward the bed and lifted her on to it as he pulled her shirt from her shoulders. Meghann shivered beneath his touch, but her fingers moved to his hair and gripped. Gently he unclasped the front hook of her bra and released her breasts, cupping them in his hands.

"I forgot how good this feels," she sighed tipping her head back.

"Surely you…"

Meghann captured his gaze. "There's been no one since you."

Readjusting, Max straddled her, looking down at her and searching her face for signs of regret. There weren't any.

"I dated three women over the years. We went to movies and dinners. Two of them I brought home. Everything always started and ended on the couch. We would kiss, and I'd send them home. Meghann, I couldn't get past us. I couldn't sleep with another woman knowing my heart was still yours. No matter how far away you were."

Her lips curled into a wide smile. "Neither of us have had sex for five years?"

Max chuckled. "We have to be two of the most uptight people walking the planet."

"Tomorrow is going to be a glorious day."

"It most certainly is," he agreed as he took her mouth again, and dove back into pleasing her.

MEGHANN RAN her fingers through the small tuft of hair on Max's chest. The light from the living room filtered through the hall and into the dark bedroom. She supposed they hadn't worried that Paige might come back to the house, because they hadn't even shut the bedroom door and they'd been at it for hours.

Five years was a long time to not have had the pleasure of another person, but she was sure it wouldn't have been pleasurable it if were with anyone but Max.

His fingers caressed her shoulder. "What are you thinking about?"

"A million things really." Meghann pressed a kiss to his skin. "Mostly about how much I enjoyed that."

Max kissed the top of her head. "We can certainly do more, but I need a few minutes of sleep."

Meghann giggled, and lifted herself up on her elbow to look at him. "Did you really make Paige stay somewhere else?"

"Don't worry about her. She's at Kennedy's. She wouldn't dare come in here tonight. I think she knew what was going to happen."

"Doesn't that embarrass you?"

"Should it?" his voice grew softer and his eyes had closed. "Isn't this what your brother sent you to my house for?"

Meghann rested her head back down on his chest. "I suppose it was. He's been the one I've leaned on throughout this whole time. I mean leaving you, and now he's been here taking care of Mom."

Max's fingers drew small circles on her shoulder again. He didn't say anything else, and the movements on her shoulder grew slower and slower until they stopped and Max's breathing deepened.

Meghann shifted to look at him. It had been a long time since they'd fallen asleep in each other's arms.

They'd promised not to think beyond tonight, but as she lay there in the silence, she couldn't help but let her mind wander to what ifs.

What if this was all they got, and everything went back to the way it was before she'd arrived? Although, it never would go back. Her mother was sick.

Meghann squeezed her eyes closed. It was inevitable, they were going to have to put their mother somewhere for her own safety and wellbeing. What were the chances that they would find a place that she fell in love with more than her own home? It was unlikely, she figured.

Max's arm tightened around her and his other hand linked with hers.

"I thought you were already asleep," she whispered.

"I could feel you thinking too hard. She's going to be fine,

Meg," he said softly, kissing the top of her head again. "We're going to see to it that she's taken care of."

She pulled the sheet up over her bare shoulders and let the sound of Max's heartbeat soothe her. She'd dragged him into her problems, and he'd made them his own. Max owed her nothing, and yet he was there for her. All she'd had to do was show up and ask.

They'd promised not to talk about the future, but she began drifting to sleep thinking about it. There was a strong pull to stay in Max's bed each night, wrapped in his arms. Perhaps New York would need some more thought.

Then her eyes opened wide, and the sleep that had been taking over her head was only a memory. Everything she'd built was in New York, that much was true. The studio, the offices, the company that owned her name. But why couldn't all of that be right there where Max was?

She'd done her time, building and slaving to create the brand. Didn't they owe her some credit to do things her way for a little while? And seriously, if they didn't, what did she have to lose? She'd amassed plenty of money to live off of for the rest of her life. But she loved what she did. People loved what she did. If they didn't want to let her film from her home town, someone else would come along and produce the show. Heck, she could be the next YouTube star. The very thought of it had her heart racing, but she lay pinned to Max, his arm holding her right where she belonged.

She'd give it more thought in the morning, but she couldn't wait to get back to New York and see what they had to say about her plan.

CHAPTER 25

They'd spent Sunday alone in Max's house as if they were hiding from the world. When she'd called Ryan to check on their mother, he'd hung up on her after telling her to take a day off. At first it had pissed her off, but when Max folded his arms around her and held her against him on the couch, she understood that she needed the peaceful moment. Oh, she knew in time she'd owe Ryan big, but for the day, she'd accept his generosity.

It was quiet Monday morning, and Meghann pulled the comforter up closer to her face to block out the light that was in her eyes.

Once she had fallen asleep, she slept soundly. She couldn't remember the last time she'd done that. After a few more comfortable minutes, she rolled over to find Max gone, but the scent of his cologne lingered in the air.

Meghann forced herself to sit up and look at her phone, which had died some time during the night. Guilt pained her heart, what if her brother had needed her?

She ran her fingers through her hair and logically thought it out. He knew where she was if he needed her.

Kicking her legs over the side of the bed, Meghann fumbled to her feet, and found the shirt Max had taken off of her. She shrugged it back on, pulled on her panties, and went to find him.

As she walked down the hallway, the scent changed to fresh brewed coffee. When she turned to the kitchen, she saw the light on the coffee maker still on and a note. The clock above the microwave read six-forty-five.

My mornings start early. But you are welcome to stay as long as you like. I'll meet up with you later. Love, Max

P.S. I left you a key to my house on the dresser. Keep it.

Meghann pressed the handwritten note to her chest. How silly was it that it made her giddy inside to know he wrote her a little note?

She felt bad that he got ready so quietly while she slept, but he probably knew just how much she needed her rest.

Meghann poured herself a cup of coffee and walked back to the bedroom. The key was right where he'd promised it would be. *Keep it*, the note had said.

Gripping it in her hand, she let out a sigh. She had a lot to do today, to change the course of her life.

It was almost seven o'clock, and she'd be taking advantage of her brother if she didn't go straight home, but she knew Paige had a yoga class at seven-thirty. Wouldn't that be the perfect start to a new day?

Meghann looked at the key in her hand. The perfect start to a new life.

PAIGE HAD HUGGED Meghann tightly when she'd arrived at the yoga studio, and smiled as if she knew a secret no one else knew. Meghann supposed that was exactly the case. Or maybe she smiled because Meghann looked as happy as she felt.

Either way, stretching and breathing her way into the day was the perfect start, she thought on her way home. Maybe she would stop and pick up something for breakfast for her brother and mother. Then again it was almost eight-thirty and they'd have long ago had breakfast.

When she pulled up to the house, Ryan's car was gone. Certainly he hadn't left their mother home alone.

Meghann parked, and as she climbed from the car and skirted the front, she realized she was a good foot from the curb, but if her mother was home alone, it didn't matter how she'd parked.

She pulled her key from her purse as she ran toward the door. Unlocking it, she pushed it open.

"Ryan? Mom?" she shouted, hurrying down the hallway. They'd been there not too long ago, she could still smell bacon. "Mom?"

And as if they knew she was looking for them, her phone rang with Ryan's ringtone.

"Where are you? Where's mom?" she answered, now out of breath.

"She had a doctor's appointment early this morning, and that's where we are."

"I didn't know she had that."

"Some things were scheduled and happened before you managed to get here. Point is, you need to come down here. They need to talk to us."

Meghann reached for the stair railing and lowered herself onto the first step. "She's worse, isn't she."

"Do you want me to keep you on the phone and tell you things you already know, or do you want to get your ass down here and talk to the experts?" he kept his voice even, and slightly hushed, which told her their mother was nearby.

"Can you text me over the address? I'll head out right now."

"Okay, and hey," his voice softened, "it's all going to be okay. Just tell me you had a nice night."

Meghann laughed as the tears threatened to roll down her cheeks. "I had a wonderful night."

"Good. I'll see you soon."

The call was disconnected and Meghann sat on the stairs for another moment to collect herself.

How would she ever repay her brother for being there for her and their mom the way he had?

Meghann freshened herself up after her tears, and changed out of her yoga clothes.

As she locked the front door, Max pulled up in front of the house.

She waited as he climbed out of his truck.

"Headed out?" he asked as he moved to her and placed a gentle kiss on her lips. "You don't look so well."

"I was hoping to look better," she chuckled and leaned into him. "Mom is at a doctor's appointment and Ryan wants me to come down. They want to talk to us about her."

"And you're worried?"

She eased back. "Of course."

"Do you want me to go with you?"

Meghann shook her head. "I'll be okay. Are you here to fix something?"

Max nodded. "I have a new toilet, stuff to tack down the carpet and there was a corner of the flooring in the kitchen coming up I was going to tend to. I have a guy coming by to look at the fence, specifically the gate. Is there anything else that you want me to tend to?"

"No." She handed him her key. "I don't know how long we'll be."

Max took the key and dropped it into his chest pocket. "I'll lock up if you're not back. You guys call me, and I can have dinner ready for you too."

Meghann gazed into those warm, dark eyes. "I love you, Max. These are the little reasons I do."

"I love you too. I'll help you get through this."

She took his hand and gave it a squeeze before walking to her car.

As she opened the door, and got situated, Meghann watched Max pull his tools from his truck.

Her heart had tumbled right back in love with him, perhaps even more in love with him than she was five years ago. There was no way she could ever go back to New York for good.

When she'd gone to him the week before, she never would have imagined that they would fall right back in sync. Now, she never wanted to let that go again.

CHAPTER 26

Ryan sat in the waiting area of the medical facility, alone. The moment Meghann saw him, she began to cry, there was no holding it back.

He rose and walked to her, enveloping in his arms.

"Why are you crying?" he asked, holding her tight.

"What do they want to say? Why do they need to talk to us?"

He eased back and Meghann wiped at her eyes. "She's not doing well, Meg. And neither of us are trained to take care of her. They want to tell us our options."

"Our options? As in what suits us?"

"You can't think that you can do this. I can't do this."

"She's our mother. We owe it to her to try."

Ryan took her hand and guided her back to where he'd been sitting. "You've been here a week. Look at everything she's been through in just that week."

"Are you saying that I wasn't capable?"

Ryan ran his hand over his hair. "You're picking a fight. Stop. Listen to me. I've been here. I've been here the whole time. When Dad died, she started to slip from us. But it wasn't dangerous or concerning. At that point, she was mostly lonely. In the past six months, it's taken a turn."

"Why didn't you tell me how bad it was?"

"Why? What could you have done from New York? I told you what was going on."

"I didn't realize she'd gotten this bad."

"Now you know." Ryan leaned back in his seat. "You can't give up your career and I can't give up mine. And neither of us are trained to take care of her. But there are facilities with staff that are trained to take care of her. It doesn't mean we gave up or are giving up. It means she's in good hands and we are mentally better off to spend quality time with her here. Do you understand?"

Of course she understood, but the guilt that plagued her was making her sick.

"She'd never lock us up in a home," Meghann argued, wiping away more tears.

"Okay, let's look at that. Imagine we were small, and Dad wasn't around. What if one of us had challenges that could get us hurt, or hurt others? What if one of us could be cared for by experts? She'd make sure we were taken to the experts. And she'd be there for us. Think about it, Meg, we have to do what's best for her. We have to give her a life of comfort and safety. No matter what Max does to the house to keep her safe, she's still going to wake up in the middle of the night and think it's thirty years ago. What if she opens that front door and walks right out? What if she walks away from that stove? What if—"

"I get it," she interrupted. "I get it."

"Don't you think, when her mind is clear enough, she's sad that neither of us are doing what we love to do, because we're following her around the house all day? She loves watching your cooking show, especially when you say 'my mother always does this or that,'" he used his fingers to quote. "She's so proud of you, Meg."

"Ryan, I don't think I can go back now."

"Because of her or because of you?"

And wasn't that the real question? "I want to be here with her. But I can't leave Max again. We've fallen right back into life like it was."

"I knew that would happen. I don't think there's a person who knew either of you who wouldn't think the same. I've never heard of him dating anyone else either."

A smile tugged at her lips. "He said he never has. Well a few movies and dinner, but…"

"But…"

She nudged him and laughed. "I have to go back to New York and make arrangements."

"Okay."

"But first, we see what they say about Mom."

Ryan put his arm around her shoulders and squeezed just as the nurse came for them and walked them to a private room.

MAX HAD FIXED the items on his list, and started on the patio when his associate had come to look at the fence. If they moved swiftly, they could have everything done in the yard by the end of the week. But he would talk to Meghann and Ryan first.

As he packed up his tools in the back yard, he could hear the cars pulling up in front of the house and in the driveway. Staying on the back porch, he allowed them through the front door without him standing there. He was worried that if Patricia saw him, she might not know him, and he didn't know what might happen then.

Ryan had his arm around Meghann's shoulders as they walked into the kitchen. Max watched as she sat down at the table and pressed her fingers to her eyes.

Patricia wasn't with them.

Max moved to the door, tapping on it before he slid it open. "I don't mean to interrupt. I was still outside and didn't want to scare your mom," he said as Ryan moved to the stove and picked up the tea kettle and Meghann stood from the chair and swiftly moved to him, wrapping her arms around his neck.

She buried her face into his chest and sobbed.

Max ran his hand down her hair and held her tightly.

"Hey, what's wrong? What happened today?" he asked as he tried to soothe her.

Meghann sobbed as Ryan filled the kettle. "She's upset because Mom can't come back here," Ryan said, his voice filled with emotion that Max assumed he was trying to choke down.

"Oh, sweetheart," he said softly as he pressed a kiss to her temple. "C'mon, tell me what they said."

Meghann eased back and looked at him through tear filled eyes. "They had us put her in a temporary care facility so they could evaluate her. But they said she shouldn't come home. Not only is her mind failing, but her body is failing too," she managed on another sob.

Max kept his arms around her. He'd get the whole story soon enough, he thought, from both of them. And he'd continue to be there for both of them for as long as they needed him.

CHAPTER 27

Meghann lay awake looking at the ceiling of her bedroom while Max snored softly beside her. The house was eerily quiet without her mother there, and yet her mother didn't make any noise at night.

Ryan had gone home, and she wondered if he, too, was staring at the ceiling unable to sleep.

She'd have hoped that exhaustion would have taken over, but it hadn't. Instead guilt swam in her belly, mixed with uncertainty. They'd left their mother under someone else's care—their frightened mother.

Warm tears fell from Meghann's eyes and she reached for Max's hand. Even in sleep, he instinctively interlaced his fingers with hers. He'd been her beacon of hope, her shining light, her strength. They could have fixed all the things in the house he had tended to, but Meghann had needed him.

In her restless state, torn between honoring her mother and staying with the man she loved, versus her career, her career was losing. Somewhere between leaving the care facility and climbing into bed with Max by her side, she'd decided that instead of asking for provisions to move production, or schedule it differently, she was ready to walk away. Meghann needed to be close to her mother, and at the same time, she wasn't ready to leave Max again.

She'd given up everything to be the name of the show—the brand. Frankly, she wasn't sure she had it in her anymore.

But as she let go of Max's hand and rolled to her side, she knew it wasn't as easy as strolling in on a Monday morning and saying she quit. They owned her and she'd allowed it.

Max's arm came over her and he pulled her closer. "Why are you awake?" he whispered in the dark, his voice heavy with sleep.

"Too much on my mind."

"Want to talk about it?"

God, she loved him, she thought as she settled in next to him. "No. I really want to sleep," she admitted.

He pressed a lazy kiss to the back of her head and his breathing deepened again.

Meghann closed her eyes and let the feeling of his body pressed to hers calm her. Later, she'd figure out what to do.

MAX STARTED his morning earlier than normal, allowing himself time to stop by home, shower, change, and brew his coffee. This morning he brewed it extra strong.

He stood with his hip against the counter, his eyes closed, and his arms crossed in front of him waiting for the coffee to finish, when Paige cleared her throat and he opened his eyes.

"Long night, dear?" she teased as she opened the refrigerator and pulled out a bottle of water.

She was dressed in her yoga attire, though he'd come to find out that wasn't just for teaching or taking class, it was a fashion.

"Meghann was restless. I didn't get much sleep, and then I still needed to come back and get myself ready."

"And her mother didn't mind you spending the night?"

Max raked his fingers through his still damp hair. "They put her in a care facility yesterday. A temporary one for now, until they find a longer term one for her."

Paige turned to him, resting her hand on his, her eyes sad. "I'm so sorry. What can I do for them? Anything?"

He loved his siblings, he thought as he smiled at her. They cared for everyone. "I'll let you know. I just couldn't leave her last night."

"I wouldn't blame you. Maybe you need to keep a bag in your truck in case you end up there more often."

She was genius. "I should do that."

"I thought Dad moving was hard enough. But he did that on his own because he wanted to. I can't imagine having to send him away."

And when Paige put that perspective on it, he knew Meghann had to be torn up inside more than she was letting on.

Max poured his coffee into his mug and tightened the lid. "Have you talked to Dad lately?"

Paige sipped her water. "I talked to him yesterday I think. He'd heard Meghann was back and he wondered how you were taking it."

"He didn't call me."

"He didn't want you to blow him off." Her brows rose. "You tend to clam up over things like that where Dad is concerned."

That he did. Besides, Paige had always been closer to their dad, since he'd mostly been her only parent, after her mother had died when she was only six. In fact, he hadn't given a lot of thought to the fact that maybe Paige was lonely without their dad in town. Had Max given her enough attention to help her through that? Probably not. Max only ever thought of his business and his next projects. He'd made his life one big routine with paperwork at the end of it. Really, that wasn't any kind of life was it?

"I'll try to let you know where I land," Max told Paige as he headed for the door. "Your walls should be dry enough to start some of the work. I'll be over there in a bit to look it over."

"Max, don't worry about my house. If I can crash here, I'll do it. Take care of Meghann first, and yourself too. You don't know if you'll get another chance to have her around. I know that's worrying you."

He smiled at his sister as he walked out of the house. Yes, it did worry him. Without Meghann having to look after her mother daily, there was no reason for her not to go back to New York and pick up where she'd left off. But this time, Max didn't want her to go without him.

As he opened the door to his truck, setting his coffee mug in the holder, he thought about the piece of paper that was tacked to the board behind his desk in his office. He'd kept it for years because the offer always stood. Maybe it was time to call Collin Avery and see if he was still interested in buying *Devereaux Construction*.

CHAPTER 28

Ryan paced the small waiting room outside the office of the therapist where they had sent their mother. Meghann sat in the corner at a small table with her laptop sorting through emails, messages that had come in over the past twenty-four hours.

"Why tell us to be here at ten if they were going to take two hours with her and leave us out here?" Ryan picked up a magazine, looked at the cover, and replaced it. "It's not like we don't have other things to do, too. Hell, we could have been touring facilities."

"But this appointment helps us decide what kind of facility," Meghann reminded him, lifting her glasses from her nose, and balancing them atop her head. "Don't flake on me now, Ry. You're my rock. The one with a steady head."

"Well, I didn't sleep well last night. So your rock is really tired."

"Do you want to go get some rest? I'll wait for her."

Ryan studied her. "You have on no makeup, your hair isn't washed, and you're not wearing contacts. Are you going to tell me you got any more sleep than I did? Or is this your disguise so no one recognizes you and wants to know what you're cooking for dinner?"

Meghann didn't have an argument. He was right. She hadn't slept well either, even with Max cuddled up next to her. And, yeah, she didn't want anyone recognizing her. When she'd run to the store on her first day there, someone had come up to her with a magazine with her photo on it. It didn't happen often, but when it did she was forced to reconcile with the fact that people did watch her every day. Magazines did write articles about her. And if she didn't get back to New York, people would forget her.

Ryan began to pace again and Meghann lowered her glasses to her nose and returned to her emails. Plans had been submitted for the next season's recipes and guests. She'd gotten a little choked up when they suggested a Mother's Day special, but she hadn't shot it down. Not yet.

Another thirty minutes passed before someone came for them and escorted them to a room, leaving them alone again.

"Do you ever feel as if you've walked into a place, and you're never going to be let out again?" Ryan whispered as Meghann ran a brush through her hair, fixed the ponytail she'd thrown in it that morning, and dropped her brush back into her bag.

"I don't think that's a question for us, as much as it is for Mom."

"We can't be persuaded by guilt, Meg. This is best."

And she knew it was, but that didn't mean her insides weren't twisted so tightly she might get sick.

When the door opened again, a woman in a white jacket whom Meghann projected to be in her late fifties, her hair a mix of gray and brown, and a pair of glasses hanging from a chain walked into the room.

"I'm Dr. Glass. I've spent the morning with your mother."

Ryan placed his hands flat on the table. "And?"

Dr. Glass set a clipboard and a file on the table before taking an open seat. "Your mother is a delightful woman who is very aware of what is going on with her."

"She is?" Meghann blurted out the question. "I mean, she's aware?"

Dr. Glass nodded. "We had a few moments where she had some memory lapses, days, years, names, and such." She picked up the file and pulled out papers with graphs and numbers on it. "We've done a lot of testing the past two days, and your mother's attitude has been positive. Often we see bouts of depression when someone is as advanced as your mother, but she hasn't seemed to reach that level."

Ryan folded his hands on the table. "Advanced. What does that mean, exactly?"

"I would assume your mother has been showing signs for quite some time, and in her medical records there are notes that lead us to believe she'd questioned this over the years. But the stage she's in now, not only will her memory likely continue to slip, but that will begin to affect her health as well."

Dr. Glass turned the papers toward them. "Alzheimer's affects how people do things, obviously, and how they remember things. But, eventually, it will begin to take a toll on her health. As you've already seen, her walking is compromised. She said she sometimes walks with the walker."

"Yes, she's unsteady," Ryan agreed.

"Things like that will progressively get worse. You can already see that in her dental hygiene, which could affect the heart."

Meghann pressed her fingers to her eyes and Ryan reached for her arm.

"I'm okay," she said, wiping away the tears that had formed. "So what are your suggestions?"

Dr. Glass sat back in her chair and crossed her legs, resting her hands on her knees. "Unless she has twenty-four hour care, and I would suggest professional care, I would suggest looking into a facility that specializes in care for those with Alzheimer's and memory care."

Ryan ran his hand over the back of his neck. "That's what's going to be best for her, isn't it?"

"I do recommend it. Caring for a loved one at this stage is hard enough. In a memory care facility they are cared for and looked after. They are safe and fed. Often our patients come to us malnourished and dehydrated because they forget to do those basic things."

Meghann exchanged looks with her brother and then turned toward Dr. Glass. "What do we do now? Where do we look to put her? Where will she be until then? Is she going to be mad at us?"

Dr. Glass leaned in, resting her arms on the table. "I think it's best if she stays for observation until you find a place in the next day or so. Most facilities recommend that you move her furniture, bedroom, and a few pieces from home, into the her room at the facility. This will help her adjust."

Meghann crossed her arms in front of her. "Well, I guess that's it. Mom never gets to go back to her house."

CHAPTER 29

Max had paced circles around his house since he'd gotten home from work. He'd called Meghann all day and it went directly to voice mail each time. Then, his texts would go unanswered. It was nearly four o'clock when Meghann finally answered his call with a curt, "I'm too busy to talk. I'll call you later."

Now it was nearing eight o'clock and he hadn't heard from her at all. When he'd driven by her house, no one was home. He'd even driven by Ryan's house, and no one was there either.

He knew it meant that things with their mom had taken a turn. Max was a patient man. Almost too patient at times. If she needed space, he could give it to her. What was a day when he'd given her five years?

Paige walked through the kitchen and pulled open the refrigerator, pulling out a yogurt. She watched him as she crossed the room and pulled a spoon out of the drawer.

"What are you moping around the house about?"

He watched her pull the lid from the yogurt and lick it before throwing it in the trash.

"I haven't talked to Meg all day. I want to support her and be there for her, but the only thing she had to say to me was she was too busy."

Paige nodded slowly as she took a spoonful of yogurt and licked it off the spoon as if it were ice cream. "She's hurting, Max."

"I get that."

"I lost my mom when I was almost too little to realize the impact. If I'd had another thirty years with her, I can't imagine having to say goodbye to her or watch her get ill."

Max watched his sister process losing her mother as she took another bite of the yogurt. "You seemed to handle Dad's heart attack just fine."

Paige chuckled and took another bite. "Did I? Or is that what you saw?"

And that tiny statement made him feel small. Was he so caught up in his own emotions, he'd never noticed that Paige hadn't handled it too well?

"I'm sorry if I was insensitive."

Paige shrugged. "No one was insensitive. Everyone handled it in their own way. I was freaked out. He's my only parent. Aside from all of you, he's all I've ever had. And when you all had your lives to live with your moms, I only had dad."

"Paige…"

She shook her head and waved the spoon in his direction. "Don't go getting sentimental on me, Max. I'm just saying she's hurting and lashing out is how she deals with it. You know that. We all know that."

And that much was true, he did know that. It was when he bought into it that they would have problems. Meghann would come to him when she needed him, but he would make sure she knew he was there when she was ready.

. . .

MEGHANN RANG the doorbell at nine-thirty, and hoped that Max wouldn't lash out at her when he opened the door. And she thought that she was just projecting. Hadn't she been the one who yelled at him when she'd finally answered the phone, and not the other way around?

She'd sat in her car for nearly ten minutes trying to decide if she should even approach the house, but the TV flickered inside, and she knew it would be okay.

When the door opened, Meghann forced a smile to her face when it was Paige that stood there.

"Oh, you do not look good," Paige said moving right to her to gather her in her arms. "Are you okay?"

"Long day," Meghann said appreciating the sisterly affection.

"Come in. He's in his room doing book work. He didn't like listening to my TV show while he was working at the table, and I took over his home office," she chuckled.

Before they even made it to the end of the hallway, Max opened his bedroom door.

"I thought I heard you," he said looking at her. "Are you okay? You look worn out."

Paige gave her another squeeze with the arm that lingered around her shoulders. "You're in good hands now."

Max held out his hand to take Meghann's, and closed the door behind them when he'd pulled her into the room.

The moment the door was closed, Meghann fell against him and sobbed.

"It's not safe for her to go home again. She doesn't even get to go home."

Max pressed a kiss to the top of her head and ran his hand over her ponytail. "Meg, I'm sorry."

"She should have gotten a say."

"She trusted you both to make that call."

Meghann eased back to look him in the eye. For some reason that brought a calm to her she hadn't had in days. "You're right."

"I don't know how she took it, but I know she would trust you and Ryan to do what was right for her—and for both of you."

Meghann leaned into him again. "I came here tonight thinking you were going to be too mad to talk to me. How come you have all the right answers?"

Max tightened his arms around her. "I don't have the answers. But Paige reminded me that everyone deals with things in their own way. Rational seems to be mine."

Meghann chuckled. "You are always rational."

"Even when my brother punches me in the face out of jealousy, I keep a cool head."

She had no idea what he was talking about, but his matter-of-factness made her laugh. "Why would your brother do that?"

"Because I walked into the bar with my arm around Hillary, before I knew they'd had a thing."

"He thought you were moving in on his woman?"

"I guess. Took me out back of the tap house and punched me. But don't think I took it. I knocked him on his ass and punched him right in the gut as we both sat in the snow."

"Rational. You didn't keep beating him up."

Max placed his hand on her cheek. "No. I didn't. But sometimes I think I'm too rational. I let you just walk away from me five years ago. I don't think I'll be as calm this time."

"Let's discuss that another day, okay? Right now, I just need some comfort."

"And you came to me for that?"

Meghann cupped his face in her hands. "You are the only person who could comfort me through this, Max. The only one."

CHAPTER 30

W hile Ryan took the job of explaining to their mother her new situation, Meghann worked frantically to get items together that they could put in her room so that when she arrived, it was most like home.

Max had arranged for them to use one of his company trucks, and Chase, Oliver, and their brother-in-law Joel all met at the house to move furniture.

"The bed, the dresser, that box of clothes, and there is a bookcase and a rocking chair in the living room." Meghann pointed to the items she needed disassembled and put into the truck.

Max had brought in his bucket of tools and each man began working to get the bedroom moved as quickly as possible. Not one of them stood and watched the others work or asked questions as to why one item and not another. They were there to help Meghann ease her mother into a new life.

She had taken another box and added photos to it. A family photo of the four of them when they were much younger, a photo frame of her parents when they were married and at their fortieth anniversary. Ryan and his dog, and she stood studying the photo of her and Max that had been taken at their engagement party.

"That was a good night," Max's voice came from behind her.

She looked over her shoulder to see him coming toward her. "It was a good night."

"You don't have to pack that one for her. It's okay if she doesn't remember me."

"I think it is important. If she remembers at all, I want her to think about me being happy. I was happy here."

Max took her arm and turned her to him. "I want to know, aside from all of this that's happening with your mom, that you're happy now."

"I want to think that I'm happy, but, Max, we know this isn't going to last. I have to go back."

"If it could last, would you be game?"

"Game to what?"

"I'm just saying, if you could have everything including your career and us, would you take it?"

"I don't know how that's possible," she said as she bit down on her lip. "But yes. Of course I would."

Max leaned in and pressed a kiss to her lips. "That's all I wanted to hear."

When Patricia Carr's room had been set up, the bed made, and photos arranged, Meghann hugged each of the men goodbye and thanked them for helping.

Chase kissed her on the cheek. "If you, your mom, or your brother need anything, and I mean anything, Hillary and I are just a call away."

"I appreciate that. I really do."

Chase shook his brother's hand and walked out with the other men.

"I owe them a nice dinner or something for doing that last minute," Meghann said as she turned to the dresser and reorganized the photos one more time.

"They don't need payment, though they won't turn you down. But they did it for you."

"Ryan said she took the news okay, but then asked if my dad would be here too," Meghann said staring at the photo of her parents on their wedding day.

"She'll adjust."

"She will. Like you said, she trusts us to make the right decision for all of us."

"And you've done that."

"I think we have. There's a hair salon down the hall. They have an ice cream parlor that's decorated for birthdays. They'll feed her three meals a day and make sure she does activities. It's the right thing," she said but she heard the questioning in her voice.

"It's the right thing. And I know you still have a lot to do today and tomorrow, but since she'll be okay here and safe, I still want to spend the weekend with you at the cabin."

"Oh, Max, I don't—"

"Please think about it."

Meghann turned and leaned into him, letting his arms come around her and hold her. "Okay. And then Sunday, I have to go back to New York."

Max eased back. "You can't extend your stay?"

"I thought I could finagle more time, but time is money, and schedules are set, and—"

"And you're under contract to keep producing. I understand."

"I'm sorry."

"Don't ever be sorry, Meg. We have the time we have, and you've told me everything I need to know."

She didn't remember telling him anything, but she didn't have time to think about it either. The door to the room opened and

Ryan and their mother walked in with the manager of the facility and a nurse.

"Hello, Meghann," her mother said and smiled as she held out her hand to her.

The nurse held the walker as Ryan held their mother steady.

"You look good, Mom."

"It's been a long day. I just want to take a nap in my own bed."

Meghann stepped back and Ryan helped their mother to her bed. She looked around the room as if she recognized it, but exhaustion was taking its toll on her, and Meghann wondered if that was for the better. Though she wondered if she realized this wasn't her bedroom at home.

"Do you want me to sit with you?" Meghann asked as her mother laid back on her pillow and the nurse moved in to put the walker close to the bedside, but out of the way so it wasn't a danger to Meghann's mother.

"That's silly of you to ask. You have things to do, a TV show to appear on. Max, make sure she takes care of herself," her mother said and Meghann turned to him to see his eyes wide, but then a smile formed on his lips. "I'll be just fine here in my bed. You all can go now."

Meghann leaned in and kissed her on the cheek and Ryan did the same. As they started for the door, her mother held out her hand for Max.

Max moved to her bedside and placed his hand in hers.

"Don't give up," she said before she closed her eyes and let go of his hand.

CHAPTER 31

Meghann pressed her back to the wall in the hallway and covered her face with her hands. "I'm confused. She's all mixed up at home, and here, she has everything in order?"

Ryan moved in and pulled her to him. "She's gone through a lot today. This isn't what she wants to do, but she won't disagree with what we choose."

"Then we should take her home."

"No," Ryan eased back and gave her a stern look. "She needs to be here. For this moment she knows all of our names. She knows Max. She knows she's sleeping in her own bed. Tomorrow may be completely different. In a month it might be a different game all together. We don't second guess our decisions here."

Meghann thought about what Max had said. "She trusts us to make the right decisions."

"And we did. For all of us."

Meghann nodded and wiped her hand over her wet cheeks. "We did."

"Now, they're going to let her rest. Then they're going to make sure she's awake for dinner. She'll have a good meal. They have a choir coming to sing for them tonight, and she's always loved choirs. I'm going to go home, walk my dog, and eat junk food on my couch. Go home with Max. Go to his house. Let's not go back to her house tonight. Let's just give us all a night to process."

Meghann wrapped her arms around her brother's neck. "I love you. You still are my rock."

He chuckled in her ear as he gave her one last tight squeeze.

MAX REACHED for Meghann's hand as they walked out of the building and toward her car.

"It's Thursday. Maybe we should go to the tap house. It's trivia night," he offered.

"I don't know."

"I think it would do you some good. I know everyone would like to see you."

"I feel guilty leaving her here and going out."

Max stopped and turned Meghann toward him. "And don't you suppose she felt guilty with you hovering over her twenty-four hours a day? She wouldn't want you doing that and she wouldn't want you to stop living."

Meghann eased against him and rested her head on his shoulder. "I'm so glad I tracked you down that morning. I was so nervous I was sick. But you've been the voice of reason in my head since then."

"You were nervous to be around me?"

"Of course," she said easing back to look into his eyes. "You could have turned me away, and you would have had every right to."

Max pulled her in and held her tight. "I would never turn you away. I've spent five miserable years refusing to get over you. I know you're going back, but I have this time. And damnit, I'm going to make it work this time."

"My schedule is harsh."

"And I'm in a position to make it work so that I can be with you."

Meghann wrapped her arms around him. "I love you, Max. If something derails, always know how much I love you."

She heard him sigh before he kissed the top of her head. "I love you. I always have, and no matter what happens, I know I always will."

MAX STOOD in line at the taco truck. As the weather got warmer and the days longer, trivia night at the tap house seemed to grow more popular. There were seven people in line ahead of him, and because he could, he'd bypassed the line inside to pour his own beers, otherwise, he'd have been waiting another twenty minutes there too.

As he walked back to the table with their food, he'd seen Meghann walk out the back door with her phone to her ear. He hoped nothing had already gone wrong with her mother. She needed one good night without worry, and he wanted to give her that.

He'd confirmed their reservation for Saturday, and he hoped she could relax and enjoy their weekend. She'd already told him she would have to leave right after, and head back to New York. Though, Max wondered if there was some way she could buy more time, knowing the last thing Meghann would want to do was leave when her mother was just getting settled.

Max sat down at the table and watched the first trivia question pop up on the monitor. Paige yelled out an answer, but Max's focus was on the back door.

"Give me that thing if you're not going to put the answer in," she shouted at him as he handed her the control box. "Ten seconds too slow," Paige complained.

Max kept his eye on the back door and watched as Meghann slid her phone into her purse as she walked toward the table.

"Everything okay with your mom?" he asked as he stood and pulled out her chair.

"Mom? Yeah. She's fine."

"Something else wrong?"

Meghann shook her head and then looked up at him with a tight smile. "It's all good. I have a day full of online meetings tomorrow, that's all. I'll need to carve time out to go see Mom, and I guess pack my things."

He wanted to think she meant for the their trip, but he was afraid she was thinking farther ahead than that.

Max pushed the tray of food in her direction. Suddenly he wasn't very hungry. Picking up his beer, he took a long sip. He only had a few more days with the woman he'd always loved. He wasn't willing to not spend the rest of his life with her—not this time. Sacrifices had to be made, and if she was going back to New York, and he was the one wanting things to work, then he was the one that was going to have to make those sacrifices.

Paige pushed the tablet toward Meghann. "You know this one. I know you do."

Max looked up at the screen at the cooking question and Meghann keyed in her answer. Yeah, her life was far away from trivia nights with the Devereaux family, and he was desperately going to miss those nights.

CHAPTER 32

The house was dark and void of happiness, Meghann thought as she pushed open the front door. Though she wanted to sleep in Max's arms and let him soothe away the pain of the day, Meghann had felt as if she needed to be alone.

Turning on the light in the entry, she stood there for a moment and the tears began to well in her eyes and then fall. Her mother would never step foot into her own home again, and Meghann and Ryan had made that choice, not her.

Meghann's lips trembled and she pressed her fingers to them. What had they done?

She dropped her purse on the floor and climbed up the stairs, taking each one as if there were a hundred pound pack on her back. The tears blinded her, but she knew her way around the house better than she knew anything.

Pushing open the door to her room, the pink paint and dainty flower wallpaper she'd once chosen didn't soothe her. Instead, the beauty of the room only made her feel more guilt.

Meghann fell onto her bed and sobbed. She'd locked her mother away and was about to leave her in a facility and go back to New York. And she was going to leave the man that she loved —had always loved—again.

The production company was making demands of her that she wasn't sure she could follow through on. They had a contract for a new book, twenty more shows, a kitchen utensil line, and an appearance at the food festival in Aspen—and that was just what she'd gotten out of the telephone call she'd taken at the tap house.

Sure, her bank account was full and fat, but her life was about to take a hit.

Did Meghann Carr still care about *Dinner Dishes*? Was it worth the pain and anguish it was causing? Was it worth more than a marriage and a family of her own?

She rolled over and buried her face into her pillow. There were some big decisions to make—New York or Max. Really there was no choice. She knew what she wanted. She just wasn't sure she could follow through with it.

MAX OPENED cabinet doors and let them slam as he moved through his kitchen, not even sure what he was looking for.

"Some of us, and that includes you, have to be up super early tomorrow to be at work. So why are you in here slamming things around?" Paige appeared in the doorway asking questions that to him were obvious.

"I'm sorry. I'll be more quiet." He folded his arms in front of him and leaned against the counter. "She leaves on Sunday." The words were curt and blurted out on a hard breath.

"I heard. And you want her to stay?"

"Of course I want her to stay. But in reality, I think I have to go."

Paige inched her way into the kitchen slowly to stand across from him, her back to the refrigerator as she mimicked his stance. "You have to go?"

"If I want this to work, I have to go to New York."

"You'd give up everything here to go there?"

He unfolded his arms and threw them up in the air. "What choice do I have? I love her. I have always loved her and I've been absolutely miserable for the past five years without her."

"It seems like you're miserable now."

Max turned and laid his hands flat on the counter. "I am miserable," he admitted. "I've worked too hard to walk away, but so has she. I can't go through the same heartbreak again, Paige. I just can't do it."

"You love her that much?"

"That's no secret."

His sister moved to him, placing her hands on his shoulders, and her cheek to his back. "I hope someone loves me this much someday. Enough to give up everything he's worked so hard for and his family."

"I'm not giving up my family," he countered.

"You're willing to move away from us." She stepped back and when Max looked at her, her eyes were wide. "Dad must really love Gloria," she said as her mouth fell open.

"We went from my sob story to Dad?"

Paige lifted her eyes to his. "It just hit me, that's all. Dad gave up everything he had here, and moved away from the four of us to have an adventure with a woman he'd just met."

"I was there for that," he reminded her.

"I mean, what are we missing out on by staying here? Is there more out there, but our sense of security is here so we don't know that? Maybe you belong in New York. Maybe you should have built *Devereaux Construction* among the high rises in a bigger city. Maybe I should have been teaching yoga on the beach in California."

He was beginning to wonder if she'd drank too much at the tap house. "Now you're moving too?"

"No, you buffoon. I'm saying I'll miss your sorry ass when you move away." A smile curled up the corner of her mouth.

"You think I should go?"

"Like you said, do you have a choice? Not if you want to be with her forever, and there isn't a soul in this town that doesn't know how you feel." She moved in and wrapped her arms around him. "You could be a stay-at-home dad that trades his construction hat in for building fancy playgrounds in back yards."

He chuckled as his arms pulled his sister in tighter. "I'm going to ask her to marry me again."

Paige eased back and looked at him. "And you moving is what will seal the deal?"

"I'm not going to mention it yet. She might say no the first time, but if I just show up there, bags packed, she won't say no twice."

Paige chuckled. "Only Max Devereaux would look forward to a woman telling him no to a marriage proposal, just so when she said yes it was sweeter."

"I love her. I love her so much it hurts."

Paige kissed his cheek. "I'm going to miss you."

CHAPTER 33

Early morning sunlight filled the kitchen as Meghann waited for the coffee to brew and her laptop to boot. She'd braided her hair and put on mascara and lipstick so that she wouldn't look as tired as she felt.

The moment the coffee machine beeped, alerting her that it had finished its job, Meghann noticed the alert that her video call was waiting. Pouring herself a cup of coffee, she then slid onto the chair and opened the camera on her laptop.

"Meggie!" Rick Desmond all but squealed at the sight of her, calling out a shortened version of her name, only ever used in the book she was named after. "You are a sight for sore eyes. How's your mama?"

Meghann sipped her coffee and bit down on her lip to try and push back the tears that threatened. If she fell apart in front of Rick, it would be okay. But they weren't the only people that were going to be on this call, so she'd save that for another day.

"We had to put her in a memory care facility," she said, and her voice was flat.

Rick's face soured and he shook his head. "Honey, I am so sorry." He pressed his hand to his chest. "I can make those guys reschedule this meeting. You don't need this shit so early in the morning."

Because Rick always had her back, she smiled. "We all have obligations. I'm fine."

"Good, because they're chiming in. Hold on."

Rick put on his half glasses and looked at the screen as if he were searching for something. A moment later, the screen was filled with faces she'd left behind when she'd run home. In front of her was her family from New York, and she hadn't realized she'd missed them too.

Four hours later, Meghann had drained the coffee pot and her head spun from the caffeine and lack of food. Her phone had been buzzing with messages from her brother that said, *I know you're busy, but call me when you're done.*

When she shut the laptop, Meghann buried her face in her hands. They had a big new sponsor for her show, more tapings, a food product line, and that meant more money and a bigger commitment.

This was what she wanted. This was what she'd given up everything for. It was all hers.

Now the tears that had threatened when she'd seen Rick's face pop up on her computer screen fell. The mascara that she'd put on to hide her tiredness burned her eyes as it dissolved and ran down her face.

Sitting there, at her mother's kitchen table, Meghann had everything she'd ever wanted. The man. The love. The career. But everything came at a cost.

There was no way, with everything at stake now, that she could force the hand of those who fed her and make them move production so she could stay near a man she loved and her mother. Though, having just gotten off of a video chat proved that the world wasn't stuck in one place, and business could be done everywhere, she knew there were just too many strings to pull.

She would need to return to New York. They'd work something out, she and Max, she thought. There would be plenty of money to fly back and forth a million times. People did it all the time. Married couples lived on both coasts and made it happen.

The conclusion she was coming too wasn't helping ease her mind. The tears still fell. As she cried it out, she just kept repeating, *it's all worth it*, in her head.

MAX SAT AT HIS DESK, tapping his pencil against the desktop, watching Chase read through the packet of papers outlining the proposal to buy his company. Even he noticed the tapping of his pencil growing louder when Chase finally took it away from him.

"You're making me crazy, man." Chase dropped the pencil into the cup on top of the desk with the other pencils. "I'm telling you, what they're offering you is decent, but seriously, why do this?"

Max leaned in on his elbows. "What else am I going to do. I'm not letting her go again. I can't."

Chase looked at the proposal that Collin Avery's lawyers had written up for Max when he'd approached him about buying the construction company. They were offering him a fair deal, but how much was the heartache of letting go of what he built worth? In terms of being with Meghann, it was worth everything.

His brother had spent years in finance, so he'd been the first one he'd had look at the proposal. Chase didn't know the construction industry, but he knew numbers.

Tossing the proposal onto the desk, Chase crossed one leg over the other and eased back in his chair. His arms crossed over his chest, he studied Max until Max was uncomfortable.

"What?" Max snapped.

"I know you love her. I get that. I get how deep it runs and it'll ruin you. You've had a stick up your ass for five years since she left." Chase unfolded himself and rested his elbows on the desk. "Hell, it would be better to get a plane and a pilot's license than to go through all of this. Seriously, she can't film that damn show all the time. Why can't you hire someone you trust to run this place when you're in New York? And can't she come here when she's not filming? I think the two of you are making this harder than it needs to be."

"I don't want long distance. I want her to come home from work and I'm sitting there. I don't want to video chat before bed each night. And what if we do make this work and we have kids? Then one of their parents are gone all the time?"

"They wouldn't be the only kids whose parents aren't always there."

"And who wants that?"

Chase had opened his mouth to argue, but must have decided he didn't have a case when he shut it again.

Max picked up the proposal. "I can build another company."

"You could."

"Dad picked up his life and moved away."

"Yep, he did," Chase agreed. "Kids all grown, no one here to tie him down, and oh yeah, retired. Big difference, Max."

"It's the right thing to do." Max tucked the papers into the drawer and pulled out a box. He slid it toward Chase.

Chase picked up the box and opened it to reveal the engagement ring. "You're going to give this to her? Your timing sucks."

Max pursed his lips. "What does that mean?"

"It means, she's struggling with all of this, just like you are. It means she just locked her mother in a home and has been around you two weeks. Two weeks. Don't you need time to decently rebuild a relationship?"

Max pulled the ring box back toward him and slid it into his drawer. "I kinda thought you'd understand."

Chase shook his head. "I understand loving someone so much you'd give it all up. I do. I shouldn't have said that."

"You're just lucky I didn't come across this desk and punch you."

That caused Chase to chuckle. "Yeah, because I would have."

"You're cheap like that. You blindsided me that night at the tap house," he reminded him.

"I thought you were moving in on my girl."

"See, you do get where I'm coming from. You do understand love that deep."

Chase let out a breath and nodded. "I do get it. I still think your timing sucks."

CHAPTER 34

Meghann pulled open the front door as Max walked up the step. She had her phone to her ear as she waited for him to come inside.

"So they'll send me daily emails and call if something happens?" she asked as Max stood in the entry noticing all of the luggage she had set out. "Ryan, I might not be here physically, but I deserve to know every pill she takes, every activity she's involved in. I can manage to be back a day or two every three weeks for the next six months."

Max's heart sank when he heard her say that. What the hell was he even thinking, he wondered? Was that the time she was carving out for her mother, and he was supposed to assume he'd get to fit into that too?

"I'll talk to you before I leave for the airport. I love you."

Max watched as she disconnected the call and tucked her phone into the back pocket of her jeans.

He should have let her say something first, but his blood was buzzing in his ears after hearing her conversation with Ryan.

"A day or two every three weeks?" He asked, his voice already elevated.

"I see you were paying attention," she snipped as she moved past him to pick up an overnight bag and sling it over her shoulder. "Are we ready?"

"What are all these other bags?" Max asked looking around.

"I have to head back to New York the minute I get back from the cabin. You knew that."

He did, but he didn't like it. "Maybe this is a waste of time. I mean, why have one more night if you're just leaving anyway? We should just say goodbye now and—"

Meghann dropped the bag on the floor and moved to him. Her eyes were icy hot, her mouth a narrow line, and her hands fisted to her side.

"You're going to write me off? Right here? Right now?"

"You're writing all of us off. Tell me you can't get more than a day or two every three weeks and I call bullshit."

"Then call it. What do you know about my life? You never made any attempt to follow me to New York or make it work last time."

Now he fisted his hands to his side, and thought better of it and tucked them into his pockets. He wasn't talking to his brother. Fists weren't needed here.

"We decided that. You and me," he reminded her. "Clean break. You go live out your dreams. I stay here and build my business. Don't you even put blame on me as if—" He couldn't go on when he saw the tears welling in her eyes. The signal threw him off, since her hands were still fisted to her side. "We're not doing this," he said reaching for her. "You're not going back to New York thinking I hate you. I love you."

Meghann resisted slightly, but then her body fell against his and he held her tightly as she sobbed.

"I'm sorry. I'm picking fights," she cried.

"I think I started that one."

"You did," Meghann chuckled against his chest. "I'm afraid to leave."

"Then don't."

She didn't say anything, but when Meghann eased back and looked up at him, he knew she was going to go.

"Let's get headed out. I don't want to miss a minute with you. I'll get you back in time to take you to the airport."

THE DRIVE HAD BEEN QUIET, and Meghann wasn't sure if that was comfort or stress.

When they drove down the tree shaded dirt road, she sucked in a breath as the cabin came into view.

"Oh, look at that," she sighed.

"Pretty amazing, huh? Paige says there are hiking trails all around here."

Meghann turned her head to look at him. "I don't want to go hiking. I have one night. I don't want to be anywhere but in your arms."

Max reached for her hand and gave it a squeeze. "I like that plan."

The tension in Meghann's shoulders eased. The night would only be as good as she'd let it be. Stressing over the fact that she'd be back in New York tomorrow wasn't going to let her enjoy her time with Max—what was probably her last time with Max.

Max pulled up to the cabin and parked in the circle drive. They both stared at the rustic beauty.

"When I think cabin, this is not what comes to mind," he said craning his neck to take it in through the front window of the truck.

"Vacation luxury for sure."

Max opened his door and stepped out as Meghann opened her door. By the time she'd swung her legs to the side, Max was standing there with his hand extended to help her out. Graciously she took it and stepped down onto the loose gravel.

Pulling his phone from his pocket, Max scrolled through his messages until he came upon the one from the owners of the cabin with the lock box code. He located the box among a pile of decorative rocks, opened it, and pulled out the key. Unlocking the door, he pushed it open, and held up his hand to stop her from going inside.

Meghann watched as he replaced the key and then moved to her, sweeping her off her feet and up into his arms.

She let out a gasp followed by a giggle as she wrapped her arms around his neck. "What are you doing?"

"Carrying you over the threshold. It feels as if the moment warrants it."

"Shouldn't you save that for marriage?" she asked on another giggle, but then when his eyes went serious, she felt the pang of it right in her chest. They would probably never get a chance to do this again. She was going back to her life, and he was staying with his.

Tears began to sting in the back of her throat, but she refused to let them win. Instead, she closed the gap between them by kissing him deeply as he held her just beyond the entry to the cabin.

One night. It was all they had. One night and they had to make it memorable.

CHAPTER 35

Their bags remained in the back of Max's truck. The moment they'd opened the front door to the cabin, he'd carried her inside and straight to the bedroom.

The view from the window and the sliding patio doors was all mountainous hillside. Not a person for miles.

They'd made love multiple times, taken a shower in the enormous multi-headed shower, and sat in the hot tub on the patio while sipping champagne they'd found chilling for them in the refrigerator.

Brilliant stars twinkled over their heads once the sun had tucked itself beyond the mountains.

With glasses of champagne in their hands, draped in thick, soft robes, they lounged in each other's arms and took in the beauty of their location.

"I don't think I've ever seen stars shine so brightly," Meghann said as she sipped her third glass of champagne.

"That one vacation we took where we stayed in those bungalows in Fiji," he reminded her and she sighed.

"Fiji. I often forget we did that."

"Honeymoon suite. We'd been dating all of six months and

thought it was super funny when they put Mr. and Mrs. Devereaux on the door."

Meghann rested her head on his shoulder. "I knew then that was the name I wanted to carry."

She felt him take a deep breath when his shoulders rose and fell dramatically. Meghann lifted her head and rested it back on the lounge.

"I shouldn't have said that," she offered apologetically. "We could have had that if I—"

"We're not going to talk about what we don't have."

"Agreed. We have right now."

Max set his glass of champagne down on the small table to his side. Swinging his legs off the lounge, he stood up and tightened the tie on his robe. "I'll be right back."

As he walked back into the cabin, Meghann followed him with her eyes. A moment later she heard the familiar sound of the front door opening and the door to his truck closing.

Quickly, she swung her legs over the side of the lounge too, knocking over the bottle of champagne she'd set on the ground.

There wasn't time to even set it up. Was he leaving her there because she'd brought up their past?

She pulled her robe together and stood just as Max walked back through the patio doors.

"I thought you'd left me here," she said frantically.

"Why would I do that?" He chuckled as he moved back to the lounge and sat down, encouraging her to do the same with a nod of his head.

Meghann picked up the now empty bottle. "I spilled this."

"They have four more in the kitchen."

"I can't drink four more bottles."

"You might want to," he encouraged as she sat back down and eased against him, his arm wrapped around her shoulders.

The stars twinkled brighter as the sky grew darker. The

chirps of crickets out among the trees serenaded them as Max pressed a kiss to the top of her head.

"Fiji was what sealed the deal for me, too," he admitted, and Meghann adjusted to look up at him. "Seriously. I remember my mother telling me how stupid it was to take a woman on a trip like that, a woman I didn't know very well. I just remember thinking she was wrong. I knew your soul, Meg. No one else was ever going to fill that part of me."

"Max, I thought we weren't going to talk—"

He pressed a finger to her lips. "We made our decisions back then." Max maneuvered on the lounge so he could look into her eyes. He brushed his fingers over her cheek and tucked her hair behind her ear. "My sister has made it a point to remind me that there are planes, cars, trains, and bicycles that could carry me to New York anytime I want to go."

"True, but we have so many commitments," Meghann added her opinion.

"We do. But I think we've committed to each other again, and it's worth working on. Meg, I love you."

"I love you, too."

"I'm not willing to not be us again." Max tucked his hand into the pocket of his robe and pulled out a solitaire, princess cut diamond ring.

Meghann stared at the ring he held between his fingers in the moonlight. He hadn't said anything else. He simply held the ring between his fingers.

"Max?" she managed his name and a smile formed on his lips.

"Meghann, be my wife. We can hash out arrangements later, but I can't let you leave me again."

Meghann looked at the ring and then back up into Max's eyes. In the dark, his eyes sparkled. But she thought of what he'd said. He couldn't let her leave him again.

"Max," she croaked out his name. "I have to go back."

"I know. Let me say that differently. I can't let you not be with me again. I mean, Paige is right. New York is a plane, car, or train ride away. We're both successful, we can afford to make sure we're together. Be my wife, Meg. We did what we needed to do to become successful. Now let's be together, just like we've always wanted to be. I'll do anything to make it work."

Meghann's bottom lip began to tremble, so she bit down on it. There was nothing more she wanted than to be Max's wife. Maybe he was right. They'd already given up everything so that they achieved their success, and perhaps it was time to succeed at something different.

"You're sure you want to marry me?" Meghann asked, lost in his dark eyes.

Max shifted as he took her hand and slipped the ring on her finger. "I've never wanted anything more."

Meghann looked down at her hand, and the ring on her finger. Then, she lifted her eyes to lock with Max's. She thought of the sign that had hung on the door of their hut in Fiji, *Mr. and Mrs. Devereaux.* She'd known then that that was all she'd ever wanted.

Max lifted her hand to his lips and pressed a kiss to her fingers. "Well? What do you say?"

"I say that the only thing I've ever wanted was to be your wife. I love you so much, Max."

"So that's a yes?"

Meghann cupped his face in her hands. "Yes."

CHAPTER 36

Meghann's eyes sparkled in the moonlight, with the light catching the happy tears as she looked at the ring Max had slid on her finger. He'd been prepared for her to say no to his proposal, and that would have been okay. She'd been hesitant enough.

There was no doubt in his mind that Meghann wanted to marry him. They hadn't fallen back into a rhythm for nothing. But she'd always wonder if she made the right decision, not because of a lack of love, but because of what he was willing to give up for her.

He wouldn't tell her about the sale of his business until it was final. When he arrived in New York, he'd tell her. For now, though, that was his secret and the sacrifice he was willing to make to have her forever.

"You're beautiful," he said softly when she finally wiped the tears from her cheeks.

"I'm a mess. I didn't expect you to do this."

"I didn't expect you to say yes," he admitted and she raised her eyes to meet his.

"Max, I love you too much to ever tell you no. But I'll always worry about this working out."

"Millions of people do it. We were stupid not to before."

Meghann shook her head. "No, I think we were right to do it before. It was exactly how it was supposed to be."

He wondered if it just sounded good, or if she really believed it. Max refrained from arguing and held his fiancée in his arms while he listened to the chirping crickets and she continued to admire the sparkle of the ring.

BEFORE THEY PULLED AWAY from the cabin, having only gotten a few hours of sleep, Max texted Chase and asked him if he'd give Meghann a ride to the airport in one of his limos—one of the bigger ones where the window went up and they could have some privacy. Max thought it would be one more hour he could have her all to himself, then he could wallow in his self-pity as his brother drove him home.

There had been no doubt that Chase would agree to the ride.

As they exited the highway, Meghann slid her hand to his thigh. "Since we're not too far away, would you mind stopping by so I can see my mother? I'd like you with me."

Max gripped her hand on his thigh and gave it a squeeze. "Of course."

He took the next exit and drove to the facility that Meghann and Ryan had chosen for their mother. As he parked in the lot, they watched Ryan pull in and park.

"I didn't know you were coming this morning," Ryan called out from his truck window as Meghann climbed out of Max's truck.

"I didn't know either. I'd only planned on going home and heading to the airport. But I had some news, so I wanted to share it with Mom."

Meghann held up her hand to show her brother the ring Max

had put on her finger the night before. Ryan took her hand and examined it.

"Nice. Why don't you head in and get checked in? Max and I will be right behind you."

Meghann nodded slowly and continued her walk toward the building.

Max and Ryan stood silently until she cleared the doors, and then Ryan turned to Max, his eyes narrowed.

"Are you kidding me? You think that was the right thing to do?"

Max changed his stance, just in case Ryan decided to throw a punch at him like his brother had in the past. This time Max would be ready.

"I think it's the perfect time. I don't want to be without her again."

"Her life is completely a mess right now and you want her to host the idea of marrying you?"

Realizing that Ryan wasn't a threat, Max tucked his hands into his front pockets and rocked back on his heels.

"It won't be like last time. I've made sure of that."

"How?"

Max chewed his bottom lip. He didn't want to say much yet, but if it would set Ryan at ease about the care his sister would get, Max could share his secret.

"I have a buyer for my business," he admitted. "It's not completely final yet, but—"

"You're going to sell your business?" Ryan interrupted. "Are you crazy?"

"Crazy in love with your sister. And if this is how I have to do it—"

"You can commute," Ryan interrupted again.

"I don't want to. I want to have her in my arms every night. I want children before we're too old to enjoy them. I just want to be with her," Max pleaded and Ryan took a step toward him.

Max flinched before Ryan rested a hand on his shoulder. "That's ballsy, Devereaux. You're building half of this town. To give it up for her—well, that's ballsy," he laughed as he lowered his hand.

Max chuckled. "It's love, Ry."

"Never doubted that for a moment. What does she think of you giving it all up?"

"I haven't told her. When it's final, then I'll show up in New York. Last time neither of us were willing to fold. This time, I don't see a choice. I want this, so I'll make the sacrifice."

"You're a good man. Mom and Dad always thought so too. They knew she'd be in good hands with you."

"I appreciate that."

Ryan looked up at the building in front of them. "I don't think Mom will be around for the wedding," he admitted and Max felt the squeeze of his words around his heart.

"She's declining that much?"

Ryan nodded. "They said it's taken over. It's a shitty disease. You can't stop it. You can't find it. You can't fix it. All you can do is watch it destroy."

This time Max put his hand on Ryan's shoulder.

He'd taken a breath to assure his friend that it would all be okay, but he couldn't do it because he didn't believe it. All he knew was that he'd be there for both of them when they needed him. When the sale of his business went through, he'd have a lot of time on his hands to take care of the people who meant the most to him.

CHAPTER 37

Meghann had hurried into the building and signed in. She wasn't sure what Max and her brother had to discuss, but she was sure Ryan was sticking his nose into their business. As she waited for her clearance to go to her mother's room, Meghann looked down at the ring on her finger.

She shouldn't have told Max yes. It was irresponsible. They both had too many things going on their lives to make a marriage work long distance. But when he'd asked, it was all she'd ever wanted.

The more she thought about their lives together, the more she knew that she needed to get back to New York and lay down some laws of her own. She'd carried her investors, managers, and producers on her talent and persona long enough. She'd never once, in five years, squawked at any of their ideas, products, books, shows, or appearances. Now she needed something else, and that was a marriage to a man she loved. If she couldn't do the show from her hometown, then she didn't want to do it.

When she received the all clear to visit, Meghann walked to her mother's room. She could hear the television blaring as she pushed open the door.

"Mom?" she called, but was sure her mother wouldn't be able to hear her over the noise coming from the TV. "Mom, why do you have that so loud?"

She pressed the button on the TV and turned down the sound. Her mother looked up at her, her eyes glazed over for a moment, and then as if coming back into consciousness she looked up at her.

"Catherine, how nice of you to stop by. Are you in the neighborhood running errands?" her mother asked Meghann after calling her by her aunt's name.

"Mom, it's me, Meghann," she corrected her and batted her eyes against the tears that wanted to fall.

"Meghann, that's my favorite name from a book." Her mother smiled up at her, but she was still sure she didn't know who Meghann was.

"Yes, you named me after the main character in *The Thorn Birds*," Meghann reminded her.

Her mother's eyes widened. "Have you read it? It's a fantastic book. If I ever have a daughter I'll name her Meghann."

The tears began to stream down Meghann's cheeks and she didn't know what more to say.

The door opened behind her and Ryan and Max walked in.

Ryan exchanged glances with her and when his eyes went wide, he knew something was wrong.

He moved to their mother. "How are you doing today?" he asked taking her hand.

Their mother studied him for a moment. "You look like my husband. He'll be home soon. Have you met my sister, Catherine?"

Max moved to Meghann and wrapped his arm around her shoulders as she turned into his shoulder.

"Mom, that's Meghann."

Their mother nodded and looked up at Max holding Meghann against him.

"Max Devereaux, how are you?" she asked and both Meghann and Ryan stared at him as he pushed a smile to his lips.

"I'm good, Mrs. Carr. How are you?"

"I'm doing okay. I had lunch just a bit ago, and played some dominos last night with some new friends."

When Meghann turned back to look at her mother, her mother tilted her head and studied Meghann as she wiped tears from her cheeks.

"Meggie, what's wrong with you?" she asked and the tears began to stream faster. "Oh, honey, why are you so sad?"

Did she tell her why? Did she even bring up the fact that a few minutes ago she called her by her aunt's name? Did she question her mother as to why she could call Max by name at first sight, but didn't know who her kids were?

If Meghann left town for a day, let alone a week or a month, would her mother know her when she returned?

"You know who I am?" Meghann asked.

"Of course I do." Her mother worried her lip. "Did I forget again? I do that sometimes."

"It's okay," Meghann assured her as she moved to kneel down in front of her. "It's okay."

Her mother patted her head and took Ryan's hand. "I had a lovely lunch, and played dominos with some new friends last night," she repeated. "And now you've all come to visit."

"I wanted to tell you something," Meghann said looking up at her mother. "Max and I are going to get married."

Her mother smiled. "I thought you were married."

"No, we never got that far. That was a long time ago."

"Oh. Right. I forget things sometimes."

Meghann wiped the tears from her cheeks again, and this time no more fell. "I have to go back to New York for a little bit. But I'll video chat you every day."

"I don't know how to do that."

"Yes you do. We used to do it all the time, and Ryan will help you."

Her mother nodded.

Meghann kissed her mother's hand. "And then I'll come home and we'll have a wedding."

"I do love weddings. Don't you love wedding cake? I think it's my favorite."

"Mine too," Meghann admitted. "I have to go. I have to catch my flight in a few hours."

"You're on TV, right?" her mother asked.

"I am. You can always see me on TV."

"I'll make sure they have that channel."

Meghann stood and kissed her mother on the cheek. "I love you, Mom. I'll be back very soon."

"Ask for some peach pie when you leave. They had some at lunch today. You'd like it. So would Max," she added.

Meghann reached for Max's hand and he took hold of hers. "I'll see you soon, Mom," she said one more time before she turned and walked out of the room.

Just as she had days earlier, she leaned against the wall, just outside the room and sobbed as Max gathered her in his arms.

"She's safe here," he reminded her, and she agreed with a nod. What more could she say? That was all her mother had left in life —her safety locked away from the outside world and not sure who her family was at all.

CHAPTER 38

Meghann pushed open the door to her mother's house. Again, it seemed empty and dark. What would they do with it, she wondered? When would they find time to take care of it or sell it?

Her suitcases remained stacked by the door as they had the day before when Max had picked her up for their night at the cabin.

For the first time all day, she smiled at the thought of their night alone with only the trees surrounding them. He'd proposed, again, and they'd sealed their future—again.

She twisted the ring on her finger with her thumb. There was an anxious buzz that rattled inside her. Meghann wanted to get back to New York so that she could break all of her contracts, just to get back to Max and her mother.

Max walked through the door. "Chase is on his way," he said as she turned toward him.

"Why is Chase coming?"

He moved to her and gathered her in his arms. "Because I thought you needed to go to the airport in style. He's bringing one of the bigger limos."

"I don't need that," she laughed as she rested her head on his shoulder. "I just need you for those last few moments."

"That's why I hired him. We can put up the privacy window and have an extra hour."

Well, he'd thought of everything.

"I'm going to walk through the house one more time and make sure everything is in order."

"I'll wait here," he offered.

Meghann walked up the stairs to the room where she'd grown up. After she'd made the bed the morning earlier, she'd pulled the blinds. It was dark, but warm in her heart as she looked around the room.

Though it didn't resemble the room she'd left so many years ago, it still had her touches.

As she walked the rooms, she ran her hands over the picture frames that lined the walls. Childhood memories, school photos, family photos at every age. And though it had taken her years to appreciate it, her mother still kept the engagement photo of her and Max prominently displayed.

The kitchen was in order and the back door secured. Water had been turned off and she'd done the same for the gas to the stove.

Her trip down memory lane ended when she opened the door to her mother's bedroom. The room was bare of furniture, as they had moved it with her to the facility. But the scent of her lingered and it started the tears flowing from Meghann's eyes. She didn't sniff them back or try to hide them. Her mother was never coming home, and it continued to break Meghann's heart.

As she closed the door to her mother's bedroom and walked down the hallway, she could see Max standing on the front porch talking to Chase.

He was all hers, and she'd promised him the same. Standing in her childhood home, suddenly she was flooded with emotions she'd tucked so far away. This would always be her home, and if she came back, it could be her home again. Those bedrooms upstairs could belong to her children. Oh, the things Max could do to the house with so many memories to make it their own.

Would he even consider it?

She'd know soon enough. Her mind was made up. She was coming home to be Max Devereaux's wife. Nothing was going to stop her this time.

CHASE CARRIED Meghann's luggage to the car and tucked them neatly in the trunk.

"He even wore his uniform?" Meghann mused as she locked the front door then turned, Max sliding his arm around her waist.

"He's a professional."

They walked toward the car where Chase moved to open the door for them. Meghann stopped and leaned in to hug Chase.

"Thank you for taking your Sunday to do this."

Chase kissed her on the cheek. "It's my pleasure. I have a bottle of champagne for you. I hear that congratulations are in order."

Meghann looked back at Max and smiled. "Yes, they are."

"I'm very happy for you."

"So am I."

Meghann ducked into the car and Max placed his hand on his brother's shoulder, appreciative of his time so that Max could have a few more moments with the woman he loved.

As they settled into the car, Max noticed that the privacy window was already up. There was jazz playing and soft lighting in the cabin of the car.

"This is really special, Max."

"Let's open that champagne," Max suggested.

He reached for the bottle and popped the cork, smiling as

Meghann laughed. He filled them each a glass, and tucked the bottle back into the bucket of ice.

Meghann held her arm out, and Max interlocked his arm with hers.

"Forever, Max."

He let out a breath. "Forever, Meg."

They each sipped from their glass, and Max searched her weary face for signs that she was happy. There had been so many emotions that had stirred in her since they'd awakened that morning in the large bed at the cabin. Max had watched her zone out in thought, laugh at his jokes, and then cry when her mother remembered him but not her. When she'd closed up the house, he'd seen the sadness in her eyes as she'd descended the stairs. Now, he could see her tremble as she held the glass of champagne. Was she having second thoughts of going back to New York? Would that change once she got settled back into her life?

Max sipped his champagne and eased back in his seat. This time it didn't matter. He'd be there soon enough.

THE DRIVE to the airport on a Sunday afternoon took no time at all, and Max was disappointed. He'd hoped for traffic, construction, anything to have made the drive take longer. Now, as his brother pulled up to the curb, he felt his insides twist. How could he possibly let Meghann go?

When the door opened, Chase stood there with his hand out to help Meghann from the car.

She handed Max her empty champagne glass and took Chase's hand.

"I'll get your luggage," Chase said as Max secured the glasses and climbed from the car.

A moment later, Chase had the luggage next to Meghann and had hugged her goodbye. Then he skirted the car to get back in and give them a moment of privacy.

"I wish I could still walk you to your gate and wait with you," Max said taking her hands in his and looking down at the ring he'd placed on her finger.

"I have a busy week, but the moment I have a day—"

"I know. I'll be right here to pick you up, too. We're going to make this work, Meg."

She nodded, but he'd seen the tears begin to pool in her eyes.

"I have to go," she said as her hands trembled in his.

"I know."

They stood there for another moment silent as if words made time move faster. But knowing departure was inevitable, Max moved in, cupping Meghann's face in his hands, and pressed a kiss to her lips.

He felt the crushing emotions of the kiss kick him in gut. When she pulled back, she reached for her luggage and walked into the building without looking back.

Max stood there watching her until she disappeared, and then even a moment longer. Would every departure feel like this? He couldn't bear the thought of it.

He thought of the proposal that sat in the drawer of his desk. Tomorrow he would finalize it and take what was offered for his business. The love he had for Meghann went much deeper than his own success.

CHAPTER 39

First class passenger lounges, free drinks, food, and nice chairs to wait in only had made Meghann more anxious. The flight attendants must have noticed her angst because they stopped by her seat every few moments until Meghann had become annoyed with it.

As the plane neared the end of its long flight, the turbulence began to shake them. Meghann had flown enough times to know that everything was under control, but she closed her eyes and gripped the arm rests. White knuckled, she prayed that it would end soon and they'd be on the ground.

When the plane dropped quickly in altitude, and the passengers around her let out cries of panic, her eyes opened wide to see the oxygen masks descend from above. Now her heart raced in fear that there was something more serious than just a little turbulence. As the plane bounced her back and forth, she reached for the mask and secured it as she'd been taught to do so many times.

The flight attendants no longer walked the aisles. They'd been called to take their seats.

They were going to crash. She could have just stayed with Max and been happy, but now she was going to die.

The plane took one more quick dive, and the passengers let out a collective scream, and then everything steadied.

Still gripping the arms of her seat, Meghann sucked in all the air she could.

Looking around, the rest of the passengers looked exactly the same. Everyone was pale and their breath labored behind oxygen masks that they'd put on out of training.

"Well, that was unexpected turbulence. Sorry for the exciting ride. You can remove your masks. Those were deployed on accident and the pressure in the cabin is fine. We'll be landing in about twenty minutes," the pilot's voice came through the cabin on the speaker.

Around her there was a mix of curses and laughter at his statement, and many noted that his voice shook too.

Meghann kept her mask on a moment longer, her fingers still gripping the arms of her chair.

Exciting—she wouldn't have categorized the earlier moments in quite that way. Exciting was when Max saw her and his lips curled into a smile and his eyes brightened. Exciting was when he took her hand and pulled her near him. Just thinking about it seemed to ease the pounding in her chest that had been caused by the fear of losing him. No, the plane ride away from him wasn't exciting. The plane ride back to him would be.

MEGHANN'S HANDS still shook as the plane pulled up to the gate and the passengers began to file out. There were some laughs over the flight, but unfortunately, Meghann heard more grumbles and curses.

She gathered her carry-ons, hiking her purse over her shoulder. She walked off the plane and down the jet bridge, willing her legs to carry her until she could reach a chair. The moment she crossed into the terminal, she sat down and took a few moments to catch her breath and stop her limbs from shaking. Solid ground was beneath her feet. Now all she had to do was face the people she'd come to see.

As she stood, a woman who was seated nearby waiting for her flight stood and walked toward her.

"I'm so sorry to bother you. You're Meghann Carr, aren't you?" The woman smiled at Meghann.

Meghann poised herself in the professional and grateful manner she had practiced for years. "Yes."

"Oh, I love your show. My mother and I watch it all the time. She's in a nursing home. She has that memory disease," she said, calling out the disease Meghann's mother suffered from without calling it a name. "But she knows you when she sees you and she talks to you, on the TV, as if she knows you."

Meghann felt the pace of her heart rate kick up again, and tears stung the back of her throat. No, she wouldn't cry. She would keep smiling at the woman who shared her story.

"I just wanted to tell you what joy you bring to me and my mom."

"Thank you. That is so kind of you."

"Would you mind signing this to her? Sometimes she doesn't know my name, but she always knows yours."

Now the tears welled in Meghann's eyes and she fought them back. Her mother always seemed to remember Max, too.

The woman handed her a pen and a magazine that had Meghann prominently displayed on the front cover in the kitchen of *Dinner Dishes*. Meghann studied the photo. It was a shoot she'd done a few months ago, before her mother's condition had forced her to go home—when her job was everything to her.

"What is your mother's name?"

"Georgia," she said smiling at Meghann.

"Georgia. That's a lovely name."

Meghann signed the cover of the magazine to the woman's mother and then handed it back to her.

"Thank you. This will mean a lot to her. And your ring is lovely," the woman added as she pressed the magazine to her chest. "Is it an engagement ring?"

Meghann looked down at her hand and thought of Max. She'd been away from him only a few short hours and she missed him terribly.

"Yes."

"He's a lucky man." The woman continued to smile at her. "I won't keep you any longer. I appreciate you signing this. I can't wait to show it to my mother."

Meghann studied the woman for another moment before she opened her arms and pulled the woman in for an embrace. As she eased back, the woman's eyes were damp and wide. She didn't tell her they shared a similar journey, but Meghann was sure that the woman could feel their connection.

Gathering her items again, Meghann walked in the direction of baggage claim. The thought of buying a new ticket and getting back on the plane tugged at her tremendously. But when she saw her assistant standing by the luggage carousel with a stupid sign welcoming her back from her stint at Banana-split Rehab she laughed. The show wasn't just about her. She hadn't even thought of the others involved.

CHAPTER 40

R ick Desmond waved his handmade sign and cheered as Meghann walked toward him. Low key was not his style. His large sunglasses were reminiscent of something he might have lifted from Elton John's wardrobe. His white pants were accented with a shiny belt, and of course a loud and colorful shirt.

He'd already collected her bags, and they rested on a cart to his side.

Of course he'd drawn enough attention to her, that four people moved to them asking for her autograph and opportunities to take pictures with her.

Meghann obliged, but her mind quickly went back to being home with her mother and brother—and Max—and to how different it was—how peaceful.

This was part of her life, and she'd always accepted it. Admittedly, without Rick's antics drawing attention to her, she might have made it out of the airport without anyone else having noticed or cared.

When Rick was ready to leave, he put his arm around Meghann's shoulders, a hand on the cart, and eased her away from those who had gathered. They walked outside to a waiting car.

As they approached, the driver stepped out of the car in his uniform to take the luggage. Meghann smiled, thinking of Chase driving people to the airport.

She slid into the car, followed by Rick.

"Oh, I've missed you," he said getting settled in. "None of this shit is fun without you here. There have been too many meetings and plannings." He pushed his glasses to the top of his head, and she noted the shimmery eyeliner he had on. She certainly had missed him, too.

Meghann reached for her seatbelt and as she clicked it in, Rick grabbed her hand.

"What is this?" he hollered as he pulled her hand toward him. "Someone put a ring on it!"

Meghann watched as Rick inspected her finger. "Max," she said and he lifted his eyes to meet hers.

"Max Devereaux?"

Nodding, Meghann pulled her hand back and looked at the ring Max had slid on her finger the night before. She'd talked about him enough the past five years, it didn't surprise her that Rick knew who he was, and most everything about him.

"And how is this going to work? You're filming the next two months nonstop and then we have book tour stops the next few months after that."

"I know. But people do this long distance thing all the time."

"You're right, people do. You and Max, you didn't."

"But we chose that. This time we're choosing long distance."

Rick took her hand and kissed her knuckles. "I'm happy for you. I know how much you've always loved him. I guess true love never dies, does it, honey?"

He was right. The love she'd always had for Max had never died, that was why everything had moved so quickly this time.

But the difference was this time, she wasn't going to let Max go. She'd give up everything else before she gave him up again.

MAX SAT at his kitchen table, a short glass of whiskey before him, untouched. His brother sat across from him texting on his phone. Chase set his phone down, and finished his drink.

"You ever going to drink that?" Chase asked and Max picked up his glass and looked at it.

"I'm going to approve the offer on my business tomorrow," Max said studying his drink.

"You don't want to do that."

"I want Meghann more." Max sipped his drink. "And don't go into the long distance thing. I want to be with her every day when she gets home from work. I want children that have both of their parents present. I want to grow old with her, not waiting for her."

Chase looked into the bottom of his empty glass. "I have a wife and a kid. I understand that now."

Max chuckled. "I still can't believe you got married and had kids before I did."

"I think that surprises everyone."

When his phone buzzed in his pocket, Max pulled it out and looked at it. "She's home," he said as he read Meghann's text. "She said there was some excitement on the plane, but she'll video call later."

Chase stood and carried his glass to the sink. "I'll head home then. Are you going to be okay alone?" he asked grinning.

"I'll manage, I suppose. But thanks for the ride to the airport and for the company."

"I'm here for you, bro." Chase rested his hand on Max's shoulder as he walked past him and then let himself out the front door.

Max continued to hold his glass between his hands. He was ready. Selling his business was one of the biggest decisions he'd ever made, and he knew it was right. It was time for new beginnings with the woman that he loved. It was time for new adventures and family—he wanted a family.

When his phone buzzed again, he looked at it hoping it was Meghann calling to tell him about her flight. Instead it was his dad.

Max slid his finger over the screen and put his phone to his ear. "Hey, Dad. How are you?"

"Max!" His father's voice rang through the phone. "I hear congrats are in order?"

Max chuckled. "You've talked to Chase?"

"Actually I talked to Kennedy."

Pushing his glass away, Max leaned in his chair amused at the chain of information. Surely Chase had mentioned it to his wife, Hillary, who was his sister Kennedy's best friend.

"Good news travels."

"It does. You and Meg belong together. I think you'll be very happy."

"I'm sure of it."

"Ya know, maybe we could have a double ceremony," his father said and chuckled on the other end of the phone.

Max ran his hand over his hair. "And why would you say that?"

"I asked Gloria to marry me. I didn't know we were doubling up on it," he humored and Max squeezed his eyes closed.

His father's engagement wasn't as shocking to him as the thought that he was engaged to Meghann—again.

His father had met Gloria on a cruise the year earlier, and they'd been inseparable ever since, even when his father suffered a heart attack and was rushed back home—Gloria had followed.

He opened his eyes. "I'm happy for you, Dad."

"She's a keeper."

Max knew that. He'd seen her first hand take care of his father. "When's the big day?"

"We're thinking of a destination wedding in Hawaii. We'll give you all plenty of notice. I know Chase and Kennedy have a lot more to think about now with the babies."

A destination wedding. Max shook his head. Leave it to his father to shake things up when Max's world was in a transitional phase.

CHAPTER 41

Noise from the lot didn't faze Max as he sat at his desk looking at the proposal for his company. He hadn't slept well, and it was starting to affect his nerves.

After his father had called, Meghann video called, and she'd looked distraught. She'd told him about the flight and the turbulence, even that masks were deployed. The very thought that something could have happened to her scared the hell out of him. During their call, Ryan had texted her to let her know their mother had fallen. She hadn't been hurt, but from then on, Meghann had been a wreck.

When the door to Max's office opened, he lifted his head, and narrowed his gaze on the visitor.

"You look like shit," Chase said, dressed in his uniform and casually walking toward Max.

"And you're an asshole. I don't have time to chat."

"And I'm the asshole," Chase humored as he sat down in the chair opposite Max. "Dad call you last night?"

"I assume he called all of us."

Chase nodded. "Hawaii. How in the hell are we all going to manage that? Kennedy's going to have to close her store because

Hillary is her back up. Joel has partners, so I suppose he can leave. I have enough drivers to cover. And, well, I guess you won't have to worry about it, will you? You'll be free as a bird here soon."

That was the goal, but why did it piss him off when his brother mentioned it?

"Why are you here?" Max asked, hoping his icy stare would alert his brother to his mood. But it didn't seem to faze Chase.

"I got to thinking about that proposal. You're selling the company, but you didn't include your lot and the building."

"No, I didn't," Max agreed. "They're a set up entity. They don't need my lot. Besides, if I sell my lot where do you go?"

Chase nodded, crossing his arms. "You didn't just keep this because I built my garage on it, did you? That would piss me off."

Max shook his head. "No. I mean, it's part of my considera-tion. So, let's just consider it Devereaux land. You have your garage here and people working out of it. I'll still have my office and building. If I come back here, I can start something new. In the meantime, I can lease it out and have some income."

"If you come back here," Chase repeated Max's words and blew out a breath. "I have other siblings that don't live in the state, and I don't think a thing about it. But knowing you're going to be somewhere else, that gets to me."

That wasn't helping Max process the commitment he was making. "All of you reminded me that there were airplanes, trains, and cars. I can use them to come and see you just as much as I could use them to visit Meghann."

"I guess we won the first round. She wins this time."

Max would always love his big brother, even if they didn't say it aloud. The choice was daunting, but he'd made it. Max was moving to New York.

MEGHANN WAITED for the car to pick her up early Thursday morning. She'd been on the phone already for an hour with her brother after her mother had yet another fall.

When her doorbell rang, she let out a yelp. She hadn't seen the text come through that the car had arrived.

She pulled open the door to see Rick standing before her. Big white sunglasses shielded his eyes, and four different gold chains hung around his neck. Looking at him brought a smile to her face. For that, she'd always be grateful for him.

"I didn't see the text come through," she admitted as she turned to grab her purse and bag.

"Your head is in a million places and has been all week. I can make them reschedule taping."

"Are you kidding me? Do you know what that would do?"

"You're the talent here. I think they owe you that."

And hadn't that been the conversation she'd had with herself the week before?

Meghann handed Rick her bag as they walked out of her apartment, and locked the door behind them.

She continued to receive updates on her mother as they drove through town toward the studio.

"Howard has a new photo layout for you to look at for the next cookbook. Prelims, that's all." Rick scrolled through his phone. "We have brand pitches next week, and tomorrow's taping has a private group coming to view."

Rick set his phone down and she could feel his eyes on her as she scrolled through her phone.

"Are you even listening to me?" he scolded.

"Yes. Brand pitches. Girl Scout Troop at the taping."

Rick chuckled. "I didn't say Girl Scouts."

"I know what's going on this week, Rick. I also know that my mother has taken two falls in the past week. My brother is trying to keep it together and pass on only good news, but there is an underlying tone to this texts and voice messages. Max isn't much different. He's called me and texted every day I've been here, but something is off. It's like things are happening back home, and I'm here missing it all."

Rick reached for her hand and tapped the ring on her finger. "You chose the madness over the location, sweetheart. You'll get used to it."

Would she, she wondered? Sure, she would. But she didn't have to, and that was the bigger picture.

When she'd left Max's side, she'd had a plan. Once she jumped back into work, the plan had been sidetracked. She was the talent. The investors had nothing without her, and they had a lot money tied up in her image. It was time for her to call the shots.

"Arrange a meeting with Scott and Don," she said scrolling through her phone again.

"With Scott and Don?" His voice took on a different tone. "What do you want a meeting with them for?"

Meghann lifted her head and smiled at her assistant who wore worry on his face. "I have a few ideas for the show. They're going to want to make some changes."

The worry faded and a smile curled up the corner of his mouth.

"What the talent wants, the talent gets," he said as his thumbs moved across the screen of his phone penning the email for the meeting.

CHAPTER 42

Max's signature bore the nerves that raced through his body. His hand shook, sweat beaded on the back of his neck, and there was a buzzing in his ears. He had just signed over his entire corporation and took possession of the check they'd issued him for consulting for a year. The payment for the company was in his checking account as a stark reminder to the success he'd had while building something to keep the thought of Meghann at bay. Now, he was free to be with her—in New York.

Collin Avery reached across the table to shake Max's hand. "I'll take good care of her," he promised.

"I wouldn't have sold her to you otherwise," Max said forcing a smile to his face. "I have the crews meeting at the lot at three to let them know what's going on and how the transition will take place."

"I'll be there," Collin agreed. "You're okay with this?"

Max rubbed his sweaty palms on his thighs. "I am."

"You always have a home here. You know that."

Max let out a breath. That was some of the selling point when making his decision. He knew Collin would take care of his business, his people, and him if he needed it.

"I'll keep you in the loop. Thank you for the generous retainer."

Collin smiled as he gathered the papers in front of him. "I've always found that the owner of a company is a valuable asset to us when we acquire them. It's worth every penny to keep everything running smoothly."

MAX DROVE through town and found himself driving right to his sister's store. The last thing Kennedy needed was his sorry ass busting in on her, but he knew she'd be there. She'd never turn him away and he could sit in the break room and have a cup of coffee—not that his nerves were going to benefit from that.

As he pushed open the door, Hillary looked at him and smiled as she ran a credit card for a woman who had three garment bags in her arms and another bag at her feet.

Max stood there for a moment and waited until the transaction was done. Then he offered his help and carried the bags to the car for the woman.

When he returned, Hillary wasn't in the main showroom, so he walked to the back where she and Kennedy sat with three cups on the table, and tea bags hanging from each of them.

Kennedy caught his eye first. "Sit," she directed him to the chair. "You look broken."

Max sat down next to his sister and across from his sister-in-law and wrapped the string to the tea bag around his finger, lifting it in and out of the water.

"I just sold my company."

There were no gasps, though maybe he'd expected some. Chase had known what he was doing, so he was sure the word had made it around.

"And now you're going to New York?" Kennedy asked as she wrapped her tea bag around a spoon and gave it a squeeze.

"That's the plan, I guess."

"You don't sound sold on this plan of yours."

"It's just a lot to take in. It's been a busy month. But I can't let Meg out of my grasp this time." Max pushed his mug to the center of the table. "It's what I want. I want to be married to the woman I love and I want to start a family." He heard the difference in the tone of his voice. It was sturdier and more confident. Yes, those were the things he wanted. Now he had enough money to make the move and take care of Meghann for a while.

"So are you going to have a double wedding with Dad in Hawaii?" Kennedy joked, but he saw the crease in her forehead form as she said it.

"I don't think we'll be doing that. I don't know what our plans will be."

Hillary sipped her tea. "Well, I already did the surprise wedding, so that's been taken."

Max laughed thinking about the barbecue they'd all been invited to in their back yard that turned into a wedding.

"I'm sure Meghann has thoughts on what she wants."

The back door to the store opened and Joel pushed open the door slightly. "Am I safe," he asked and Kennedy nodded.

Max chuckled to himself as he watched the man carefully slide through the door. During the week Kennedy often had women trying on clothes, and men, specifically were taught to not come through the back door. But it seemed as if rules could change, just like careers and paths through life.

"I just heard you sold your construction company," Joel said looking at Max. "Congratulations."

"Word travels fast."

"That's a big step. You have a job at the tap house anytime you need or want one," he offered.

And that was family, Max thought. Even the ones that married in had his back. "I appreciate it."

Joel pulled a mug from the shelf and filled it with coffee as Chase and Paige walked into the room from the showroom. Max watched as they all assembled as if it were casual, but he knew they'd all been called in to surround him with the love and support he'd come to Kennedy's looking for—and he hadn't even had to ask.

No one mentioned the company again, or him moving to New York to be with Meghann. They carried on with talk of their father's wedding, the new kegs that they were tapping at the tap house, and Paige's offer on the yoga studio at the end of the street.

Max would miss this most of all when he moved to New York. He would just have to make it a point to come back home often so that they never lost what they had.

Time slipped as they all gathered in Kennedy's store and soon he had to go to the meeting to tell all of his employees what he'd done. They'd be in good hands he knew, just like he was, surrounded by his brother and sisters, and their spouses.

CHAPTER 43

Meghann and Rick walked into the offices of the production company in Manhattan on Monday morning. She'd spent all weekend preparing her presentation to them, but in the end, after the meeting, she was walking out and going home—and not to her apartment.

She hadn't slept in three days, hardly eaten, and her stomach was twisted in knots. But she needed to go home to be with her mother and live her life with Max.

Scott, the CEO of the production company, and his partner Don stood when she walked through the door. They each scanned a look over both her and Rick before Scott reached his hand out to shake hers.

"It's nice to see you," he offered.

"Likewise," she agreed as she shook his hand and then Don's.

"Just the two of you this morning?"

Meghann nodded. "Yes. Were you expecting more?"

"Yes. Your calling of this meeting seemed urgent, I expected some lawyers and maybe management?"

Perhaps she should have considered that, but she was thinking with her heart.

"I just have some things I need to discuss. I thought I could present them to you," she said and heard the shaking in her voice.

Scott walked around the desk to stand in front of her. "Well, we have all those people waiting for us in the conference room. Since your leave of absence, we've been working on a few things."

"Leave of absence? I was gone a few weeks. I was on meeting calls, in planning sessions, and addressed every email that came my way."

"It was enough time for us to address a few things and make some new plans."

Meghann crossed her arms in front of her. "New plans?"

Don moved in toward them. "Let's go to the conference room and—"

"Why don't you tell me what I'm up against before we go in there," she demanded, dropping her arms.

Scott shifted a glance to Don and then back to her. "We feel like *Dinner Dishes* needs a facelift, if you will. We've decided to cancel the show and go with a new format. And new talent."

Meghann felt her knees go weak and Rick moved in next to her, no doubt for support, even though he would never say anything.

"You're canceling my show?"

"Our show, but yes. Now, should we go into the other room? We'll pay out your contract, but this is how the industry goes. You know that."

She did know that, but had she thought they were just going to fire her, after making sure she got back there as quickly as possible to begin production, she'd have stayed with Max and taken care of her mother.

By the time the logistics were over Meghann was fuming. Sure, her bank account was filled with millions, after they'd bought out her contract, and she was free to leave, but they'd taken her show away from her.

Rick wrapped his arm around her shoulders as they walked toward the elevator. "This is exactly what you wanted, wasn't it?"

She shot him a glare. "No. I didn't want to be fired."

"But you wanted out."

"I didn't tell you that."

"You didn't have to," he said as he pushed the button to summons the elevator. "I know you, Meggie. I've known you a long time. And I knew the moment I saw that ring on your finger you wanted Max more."

The elevator doors opened and they stepped inside.

"I think I should have had a say," she argued. "I should have been able to call some of the shots. I should have been able to dictate how it ended."

Rick let out a laugh and slid his large, white sunglasses down on his nose. "You did go through something when you went home. Honey, the world is all yours now. You're too popular and famous for one set of yahoos to call you done. Go home. Get married. Have some babies. Write more books. Don't you give up on me," he nearly shouted as the elevator came to a stop. "This is your moment. Get out there and call those shots."

Tears began to pool in Meghann's eyes and she laughed as they fell. This was why she had success in her life. She was surrounded by people like Max, her bother, and her mother. They all cheered her on at her darkest times, just like Rick was.

"I can go home and get married and have babies," she said sobbing through laughter as they hurried out of the building and to the waiting car.

"And hell, the payoff was more than worth your time. You don't have to work another day in your life."

That was true, she thought, as the driver opened the door and she slid into the car. But not working wasn't part of her makeup. It wasn't part of Max's either. They'd both built empires. She could build another with or without a cooking show.

The driver pulled away from the curb and Meghann leaned in

over the seat. "Take me to the airport," she told him and then eased back in her seat next to Rick.

"That's my girl," he said patting her leg.

"You'll come out for the wedding?"

"I wouldn't miss it for the world. And I expect to be standing with you, you know that?"

Meghann rested her head on his shoulder. There wasn't anyone she'd want more standing next to her when she married the man of her dreams. Yes, Rick would be there, and it would only be the start of great things.

She relaxed against the seat and smiled. Meghann Carr was going home for good, and never would she leave Max Devereaux's side again.

CHAPTER 44

Max's knees hit the seat in front of him. When had they made airplanes so tight? The view out his window was nothing but clouds. The man next to him snored, and the flight attendant had run out of pretzels two rows in front of him.

There hadn't been time to pack a full suitcase, so everything he was bringing to New York was in a duffle bag stored in the overhead storage. None of it mattered. He had enough in his checking account to buy a house and fill it. It wasn't important what he brought with him. All that mattered was that he would sleep in Meghann's arms that night and for the rest of his life.

As the plane began to descend, Max thought about the flight Meghann had described to him and how scared she'd been. When she'd began to cry on the phone, he couldn't help but have wondered what he would have done if something had happened to her.

The flight attendants made one more pass through the cabin, and Max looked at his watch. Meghann would be home by now, he was sure. He hadn't told her he was coming because he wanted to see the look on her face when he was standing at her door.

When the wheels hit the runway, Max's heart began to race a bit faster. It was all real now. Meghann wore his ring on her finger and she was going to be his wife. Everything they had planned years ago was about to come to fruition—only Max would be in New York.

Max pulled his duffle bag from the storage unit as the passengers began to exit the airplane. His fingers itched to pull his phone out of his pocket and to call Meghann. But it was all about the element of surprise.

FORTY MINUTES LATER, Max paid the cab driver, and stood on the sidewalk looking up at the building where Meghann lived. He took a deep breath and thought he might cry.

Max moved to the door, attempting to pull it open, but it was locked. Right, he was in New York. Things were a different here. He looked at the panel to the right of the door with buttons and numbers. Pressing the button that corresponded to the number of her apartment, he waited for her to buzz him in. When she hadn't come to the intercom or buzzed open the door, he pressed the button again. But still there was no response.

He could wait, or he could hail another cab and head toward her studio. Meghann had said they often filmed late into the night, and he knew they'd had plans for meetings and new products. Perhaps surprising her at work would be even better.

Max hailed another cab and was driven through the city. He paid the driver to wait for him for fifteen minutes just in case he had to adjust plans again.

The front doors to the studio opened when he walked up to them. It was late enough, there wasn't anyone at the reception desk, so Max continued into the building. He pushed through another set of doors which led to a long hallway.

Max walked down the hallway filled with doors. Each door was labeled. One door was opened, and when he looked inside, it was a conference room, but the far wall was windowed and looked out over the studio.

Warmth spread through him when he saw the mock kitchen where Meghann had created her dreams. She belonged here, and he knew the decisions he had made was the right one.

"Can I help you?"

Max turned his head to see a man in a bright floral shirt, thick, white rimmed glasses, and rings on most of his fingers.

"I'm looking for Meghann Carr," Max said and the man's brow rose.

"Did you have an appointment? I don't think so. Stalkers need to go back out on the street."

Max shook his head. "I'm not a stalker," he chuckled and then worried that she'd been faced with that in the past. "I'm her fiancé."

The man in front of him folded his arms in front of him and studied Max. "What's your name?"

"What's yours?" Max returned and the man looked less than amused. "Max Devereaux," he said and watched as the man's eyes widened as he lifted his hands to his mouth and Max was sure he'd even squealed.

"What are you doing here?"

Max looked around and wondered when Meghann would walk out of one of the many doors. "Like I said, I'm here to see Meghann."

The man lowered his hands to his hips. "She's not here."

"Then where is she? I already stopped by the address I had for her."

The man in front of him bit down on his lip. "I put her on a plane hours ago to head back home."

Max felt the blood drain from his face. "Home?"

Now the man's lips curled into a smile. "Engaged couples should communicate more," he said chuckling as he held out his hand to shake Max's. "I'm Rick. Meghann thinks I'm fabulous," he humored. "And she's been sick over being here without you."

"So she went home?"

"I'm going to let her explain it to you. But now I'm going to get you a ride to the airport so you can get back to her. She should be landing soon, so let's get you on a plane."

The man put his arm around Max's shoulders as he put his phone to his ear and called for a driver, telling them that, "Ms. Carr needs this passenger to get to the airport toot sweet."

Max laughed as the man escorted him back to the front of the building.

When the car pulled up, Rick shook his hand again. "Invite me to the wedding. I wouldn't want to miss it for the world."

"I'll make sure you're there," Max agreed as he climbed into the back of the car and headed back to the airport.

The day had been full of surprises. He supposed there was one more surprise to be had.

CHAPTER 45

T he airport was nearly empty, and Meghann couldn't remember when she'd been more grateful for such a thing. She all but sprinted from the terminal to the passenger pickup lane where her brother waited for her.

The dilemma between going straight to the facility to see her mother or to Max raged in her heart.

"I hadn't expected your call," Ryan said as they pulled away from the airport.

"I hadn't expected to call you." Meghann settled into the seat and rested her head against the headrest. "I got fired today," she said easily and kept her focus forward even though she felt her brother's gaze on her.

"Fired? How do they fire you? You're the show."

"I'm hired talent. I'm contracted. And now I've been paid to walk away."

As Ryan eased to a stop at the light he turned to her. "They paid you off?"

"It is what it is."

"You spent five years building that show. That's crap that they did that to you."

"Truth is, I'd planned to walk if they didn't let me move the studio here. I need to be here. I want to be with mom for as long as she has, and I want to be with Max—and he's here."

"You would have walked away?"

"I would have. Like you said, I built that show. I built the brand. I can do it again."

Ryan chuckled and shook his head. "All I care about is that you're happy."

As they drove on, Meghann thought about it. Being with Max was the one thing that would make her happy.

RYAN HADN'T GIVEN Meghann a choice of where she'd like to be taken. He'd driven directly to the facility where they'd put their mother.

As he parked the truck, Meghann looked up at the building. "I'm sorry I left you to tend to all of this," she admitted as guilt rose into her chest.

"You had to do what you had to do. But now you're back."

"And how long does she have? Maybe if I'd stayed here all along—"

"Don't do that to yourself. She would have gone through this no matter what. She's had some bad days, but she's had some good ones too. Show up every day, Meg, and no matter how long she has, she'll have something to look forward to."

"On the days she remembers."

"Well, there is that. But if you don't show up every day, you won't know if it's a good day for her or not. Don't miss any of them from here on. Maybe getting fired was the best thing yet."

Meghann reached for her brother's hand for the comfort of it. Ryan was right. It was the best thing that could have happened.

.   .   .

ARM IN ARM, Meghann and Ryan walked toward their mother's room. The door was open and they could hear their mother talking to the TV as she answered the questions on the game show she watched.

Meghann and Ryan stepped into the room and their mother lifted her head to acknowledge them. She lifted her hands toward them.

"My children," she said as they inched into the room. "Come in. Come in. I'm just watching this silly TV show. Meghann, when did you get back from New York?"

Meghann batted away happy tears. Her mother knew who she was.

"I got home just a bit ago. I'm here to stay," she said taking her mother's hand and sitting down in the chair next to her.

"That's good. I miss you." She turned her head toward Ryan. "C'mon in, Ryan. Come sit with us."

It didn't go unnoticed that Ryan had tears in his eyes too.

THEY'D SAT with her for hours, until the nurses came to put her to bed. Their mother had kissed them both goodnight, called them by name, and told them she loved them.

As Ryan drove her home, there had been silence between them. No doubt both of them holding on to the feeling the evening had given them.

As they pulled up to their mother's house, Meghann pulled her phone from her purse. She would have thought Max would have called her by now, as he did every night, but there were no calls.

"Are you headed to Max now?" Ryan asked as he put the truck in park.

Meghann nodded. "I didn't tell him I was coming. I wanted to surprise him," she admitted. "Well, I guess I didn't even know I was coming. This has been the strangest day ever." She laughed and her brother patted her hand.

"I know it stings. you worked your ass off for that show. But the timing—I can't help but feel as if it's right."

Meghann looked at her brother and savored the sincerity that came from his eyes. "I think you're right. I'll talk to you in the morning."

She climbed from the truck and went straight to her car, unlocking the door and climbing in. When she started the engine, Ryan finally backed out of the drive and drove away.

Meghann backed out of the drive as well and started toward Max's house. She couldn't wait to see the look on his face when she was standing at his door. Tears began to stream down her cheeks, but laughter escaped her throat. She'd been fired. They'd cut her loose and paid out her contract. The world was hers right now, and she was right where she wanted to be.

Maybe Max would hire her as his secretary, just to give her something to do. Or maybe she could work for Paige when she opened her studio. Meghann laughed again—the studio. Maybe she could invest in Paige's studio and they could be business partners.

When she pulled into Max's driveway, she noticed how dark the house was. Perhaps he'd already gone to bed. No, it was only nine o'clock, he never went to bed that early.

Regardless, he'd sleep more soundly with her in his arms she decided.

Meghann climbed out of her car and hurried to the door. She rang the bell, but she heard no movement from inside. She rang it again and again.

He wasn't even home.

Maybe he was at the tap house. Of course.

She hurried back to her car and climbed inside. Starting the engine, she wondered why she hadn't thought of checking there first or even his office. Then again, she could have called him, and he wouldn't have known she wasn't in New York.

As she drove toward the tap house, she laughed to herself. Sometimes the obvious escaped her.

CHAPTER 46

For a Monday night, the tap house was full. It wasn't until she'd walked inside that she realized they were all watching the baseball game on the many TVs that hung on the walls.

Max's family huddled together at the table where they usually gathered. Meghann walked toward them, and Paige was the first to see her and jump to her feet to hurry toward her and gather her up in her arms.

"Oh-my-God! What are you doing here?" Paige shouted as she squeezed her.

"I'm home. I'm back."

"So he got to you? He brought you home?" Paige said in her ear before easing back to look at her.

"No. I came on my own to surprise him."

The smile on Paige's face faded. "You just came home?"

"Well, I got fired, so I—"

"You got fired?" Paige's voice cracked. "Wait, you haven't seen Max?"

"No. That's why I'm here. I was hoping he was here. He wasn't at home."

Paige worried her lip and it caused a lump to form in Meghann's throat. "What's wrong with Max? He's not here, is he?"

Chase moved in behind Paige, holding his daughter in his arms. "Hey! I didn't expect to see you. Did you bring Max back with you?" Chase looked around the room as if looking for his brother.

"What's going on?" Meghann asked. "I haven't seen Max. I haven't even talked to him because I was trying to surprise him. I got fired this morning, and my assistant put me on a plane."

Chase rubbed his free hand over the back of his neck. "Well, that's a predicament."

"Where is he?"

"I'm here—finally," Max's voice came from behind her, and when she turned to see him, she could see the dark circles around his eyes and his face was shadowed with whiskers.

"Where were you?" she asked as he walked toward her, sliding his hands to her hips.

"In New York. I sold my business, padded my bank account, and flew to New York to surprise you. I'm all yours. I'm ready to settle down with you in your big city so that you can live out all your dreams, we can have our family, and we can be together."

Meghann's lip trembled. "You sold your company?"

"Yeah."

"Oh, why did you do that?"

Max brushed a strand of hair from her face and tucked it behind her ear before resting his hand on her cheek. "Pride got in our way last time, Meg. I can build something new again someday. Right now, all I want is you. I want us to get married and have a family. I want to grow old with you, and I want you to have everything you worked so hard for. But that doesn't explain why your assistant with the loud shirt and big glasses turned me right back around and put me on a plane."

The tears rolled down her cheeks now, and she hiccupped laughter. "You met Rick?"

"I met Rick."

"You went to New York."

"I just told you that."

Meghann pressed against him, her hands planted on his chest. "I'm home now. I'm back here to be with you."

Max eased back to study her. "What does that mean?"

Meghann wiped her eyes. "It means that my plan when I got back to New York was to see if they'd work with me. I was the talent, after all. Their brand was built around me. So, I spent all weekend working up my proposal to move the show here. I wanted to be here with you and my mom. I wanted to raise my family here. And seriously, why couldn't they film here? Right?"

"You moved your show here to be with me?" His voice cracked as he asked.

"Well, that was the plan. But before I could even propose it, they fired me."

Now Max coughed, as if he'd choked himself with words that were trying to rush out. "They fired you? They are so stupid. Why would they—"

Meghann pressed a finger to his lips. "It doesn't matter. They paid out my contract, and now I can do anything I want to."

"You're home?"

She smiled. "I'm home."

"And you're unemployed?"

Now she laughed. "My finances are more than secure."

"Right."

"But you're unemployed?" she asked, turning the tables. "You really sold your company? Can't you get it back?"

Now Max chuckled. "That's not really how it works. But let's just say my finances are more than secure."

Lifting her arms around his neck, Meghann leaned into him. "I can't believe we are standing here with nothing."

"Well, we have each other. That's all we ever wanted, right?"

"Yeah." She pressed a kiss to his lips. "My mom remembered me too," she added and Max looked down into her eyes.

"That's good."

"It was wonderful. It might not happen tomorrow, but today, she remembered me and asked about you."

"It's a good thing you're home. You know, I think we should get to planning that wedding really soon. We can have it outside. I'll build a pergola to get married under, and your mom can be there to see us get married."

"I'd like that. I'd like that a lot."

"Well, let's sit down, and you can plan it with my sisters and Hillary. They live for this kind of stuff."

Meghann rested her head on Max's shoulder. "I was just thinking. Since we're both financially able to support ourselves for a while, maybe we can finish fixing up my mom's house and bring her home. I mean, I can afford full care. Maybe it would be good for her."

Max pressed a kiss to her forehead. "Anything you want. I'm all yours."

And she knew that. She'd always known that, but he was right, pride had gotten in their way.

As they walked back to the table with his family, she laughed to herself, he'd gone to New York to surprise her. He'd sold his business to be with her. Nothing had turned out the way they'd planned, and yet everything was perfect.

EPILOGUE

After lengthy discussions with her brother, and the staff at her mother's facility, it was decided that Meghann wouldn't bring her mother home to live with her. On the days when her mother remembered her and Ryan, it was a good day. But on the other days, at least she was surrounded by others like her and those who could help them.

Just as Max had suggested, Meghann began to plan a wedding with his sisters and his sister-in-law. They had opted for a late July wedding, in the back yard of their home—the home where Meghann had grown up.

Since he'd been free from his business, Max had remodeled the kitchen and the master bedroom. Carpet had just been laid in the living room and the room had been given a fresh paint job as well.

Of course, in the back yard, decorated in twinkling lights at dusk, was the pergola Max had built so that they could get married.

Meghann's mother had come into the house to see her in her wedding dress. She was happy to be at a wedding, though today, she didn't recognize either of her children.

"You have a nice home," she said as Meghann batted back tears.

"Thank you. I'm very happy that you're here," she said kissing her mother's cheek.

"I'd better go sit down now," her mother said, taking her brother's arm and walking back to the yard where family and friends mingled.

Kennedy stood in the doorway holding Meghann's bouquet. "You look so beautiful," she said admiringly.

"Why am I nervous? This is exactly what I want."

"Because you're supposed to be nearly sick with nerves. It's part of the protocol."

Hillary and Paige moved in behind Kennedy and admired Meghann as she admired herself in the mirror. Kennedy had ordered the dress for her, and it was the perfect combination of bridal and practical. Paige had woven her a crown of flowers for her hair, and made her bouquet.

Rick sat in a chair admiring her as well. He'd picked out the earrings she wore from Tiffany's and gave them to her as a wedding gift. He would stand with Meghann as she married the man she loved.

She smiled as she looked at him in the mirror. He wore a simple suit, but she'd noticed the rhinestone buttons on his shirt and cuffs. No doubt there was a busy pair of glasses in his pocket that he could slip on after the ceremony.

"I think they're ready," Ryan said from behind the women at the door.

Each of the Devereaux women kissed her cheek and hurried out of the house. Rick stood and enveloped her in a hug.

"Honey, I've never seen you look more beautiful." He kissed her on the cheek and followed the others out of the house.

Ryan walked to her and took her hands in his. "He's right. I don't think I've ever seen you look more radiant," he said as Meghann took one more deep breath.

"She doesn't remember us," she said.

"She doesn't. But we're going to have lots of photos so that you can share it with her again on a day when she does remember."

Meghann could feel the tears stinging her eyes. "I can't believe I'm home and that I'm finally marrying Max."

"Well, you're going to marry him, only if you quit staring at yourself in the mirror and get outside."

Meghann laughed and took her brother's arm. He walked with her out of their childhood home and toward the group that waiting in the yard.

Her mother dabbed her eyes when Meghann looked at her. Perhaps she wasn't sure what she was doing there, but she was touched by the wedding and the presence of the bride. Rick sat behind Meghann's mother in a bright pink blazer with his large white rimmed sunglasses, looking as fabulous as always. As she passed by him, he blew her a kiss. Maybe it wasn't her career that she'd miss, but she'd miss him in her life every day.

When she looked toward her groom-to-be, his smile warmed her. He'd given up everything just to have this moment with her. She hadn't thought it possible, but she loved him more than she had even that morning.

MAX FELT his knees wobble when he saw her walk out of the door. Patricia's roses were in full bloom all around them, it made the perfect backdrop for him to marry the woman he'd always loved.

On the arm of her brother, Meghann walked toward him as a harpist played music. Max saw the tears in her eyes, and then noticed that her mother cried too. Just as Meghann passed by her mother, Patricia reached for her.

"You look lovely, sweetheart," Patricia said.

"Thank you, Mom."

Ryan took his seat next to their mother as Max took Meghann's hand.

"She's right. You look lovely."

Meghann dabbed a handkerchief to the tears that rolled from her eyes. "Thank you. You look handsome."

"It's happiness, Meg. I look happy."

"Yes you do."

THEY SAID THEIR VOWS, and promised themselves to one another for life. They danced with their family and friends, ate good food, and when Meghann's mother walked back through the house, she'd remembered being there before.

Just past midnight, now just the two of them at the house, Meghann rested her head on Max's shoulder as they sat on the patio, under the stars, and listened to the breeze in the trees.

He held her hand in his, both of them admiring the ring he'd slipped on her finger at the cabin, which now stood for their union.

"We did it," Meghann said.

"We sure did. Now we're just two unemployed kids trying to make it in the world."

The comment made Meghann giggle just as her cell phone rang on the kitchen table. She hurried to it, just in case it was something about her mother.

When she saw Rick's name pop up, she worried that something had happened to him on his drive to the airport.

"Rick? It's past midnight. Are you okay?"

"Honey, did I disturb anything?" he asked and then laughed.

"No. Why are you calling me? What happened?"

"Settle," he said. "I just got a call myself. Tuscan Pasta just called. They're expanding their line and they want to do some marketing."

"Okay," she drew out the word as she walked back to the patio with her phone to her ear. "I'm listening."

"More details later, but they need a new spokesperson for their brand. Commercials, print ads, and, honey, they want a weekly cooking show from your kitchen."

"My kitchen?"

"Yes, ma'am. Now, I'm not going to let you say anything else. I'm going to say goodnight. I love you, honey. I'm happy for you. And if you take this gig, I'm moving to this cute city of yours. So, you sleep on it, under him," he joked. "I'll talk to you tomorrow."

The line went dead, and Meghann lowered the phone from her ear.

"Everything's okay?" Max asked.

"Everything's perfect. I'm home. I'm married to you. And I just got a new job—I think."

Max wrapped his arm around her shoulders. "You're right. Everything's perfect. And next month we'll head to Hawaii for my dad's wedding."

"Hawaii," she sighed. "Maybe we can go down earlier and have a honeymoon."

"I like the sound of that."

"If I accept this proposal with this new company, I'll make sure I have some say."

"I like the sound of that, too."

Meghann snuggled against him. "And maybe while we're in Hawaii, we can get to work on the rest of our plans."

Max kissed the top of her head. "Which plans?"

"The family part."

Smiling, Max stood and took Meghann by the hand pulling her to her feet. He scooped Meghann up in his arms and she laughed as she wrapped her arms around Max's neck.

He started for the door. "I don't see why we should wait until we get to Hawaii."

We hope you enjoyed book three in the Devereaux Family Series, *Max Devereaux.* Please enjoy an excerpt from book four, *Paige Devereaux.*

PAIGE DEVEREAUX

With her finger on the mouse, Paige scrolled through the website taking in the sights and reading up on Oahu. As she looked at the tropical scenes splayed across her computer screen, she was making a mental list as to what to pack, how to do her hair, and where the best beaches were to do yoga in the mornings.

Paige's father had met a woman nearly a year ago on a cruise ship, and now they were getting married. And wasn't the timing perfect? In the past year, her sister and both of her brothers had gotten married too. She, on the other hand, was apparently destined to be a bridesmaid for the rest of her life.

Sitting back on the exercise ball she used for a desk chair, she picked up her cup of tea and sipped. The mint flavor invigorated her tongue and her nose.

She didn't really think too much of marriage, but she'd been inundated with it lately, that was for sure. Things had changed quickly, but when it came to Paige's life, that was normal.

Paige was only seven when her mother was killed in a car accident and soon Kennedy and Chase were living with her and their father. But, already teenagers by that time, it wasn't long before they moved out and headed off to college and then onto new things in their lives. Eventually Paige got old enough to do the college thing and then the job thing.

Still only in her late twenties, Paige was motivated by her older siblings and their ambitious career choices. Her sister Kennedy owned a stylish boutique, where Paige worked once in a while. Kennedy had married Joel, who owned a tap house with his brother and business partners—and Paige filled in there once in a while too. Chase, her oldest brother, owned a limousine service, and Max, the next oldest, had recently sold his booming construction business to marry the woman of his dreams. Now he was remodeling his wife's childhood home for them to live in.

Entrepreneurship was in her blood. For the past year, Paige had been working and saving to purchase the wellness center where she taught yoga. Her vision was to expand the yoga studio and bring in massage therapists. The woman who currently owned the wellness center was waiting for Paige to make her offer, but she knew time was slipping away. If she didn't come up with the money soon, the current owner just might offer the business to someone else.

Paige could borrow the money from her siblings, but there was some pride in doing it all herself—no loans. Though each of her siblings, and their spouses, had offered to carry her.

As Paige clicked to the next tropical photo she let the mixture of her emotions stir in her chest. There was nothing she wanted more than a nice vacation in Hawaii in November. And she was thrilled for her father, who had finally found a woman he loved enough he wanted to marry her. On the other hand, was the man crazy for planning a destination wedding?

A destination wedding in November wasn't helping anyone. She knew the scheduling challenges it was bringing to her siblings. Kennedy and Joel had to adjust their businesses and think of taking a one-year-old to Hawaii. Chase and his wife Hillary were in exactly the same boat with his business and their daughter. Max and his wife Meghann were settling into newlywed life. They didn't have children yet, but Meghann had just been offered a new contract to promote some pasta brand, which included a new cooking show. This time, however, Meghann was calling the shots, so maybe Hawaii wasn't as daunting a thought or task as it was to the rest of them.

For Paige, it meant paying for a trip and days without work. That certainly wasn't helping her bankroll.

She sipped her tea and when her cell phone rang, she glanced at the screen before making a move to pick it up. The face of Oliver, one of her brother-in-law's business partners at the tap house, popped up on the screen and made her laugh. They'd gone for a hike together once, and he'd worn the silliest of hats. She'd snapped the photo when he wasn't looking and set it for his contact photo. Whenever he called, she got a good laugh out of it.

Paige picked up the phone and swiped her finger over the screen.

"Hey, Oliver. What's up?"

"How'd you know it was me?"

She laughed. "Seriously?" Sometimes she didn't know if he was serious or not. The noises from his end of the call told her he was at the tap house. No doubt on a Saturday night they were busier than the rest of the week.

"Tell me you're not busy right now, or out on a date, or already in bed."

"It's seven o'clock. I'm not in bed."

"On a date?"

"Almost never on a date."

She heard a man place his order and a woman laugh in the background.

Oliver cleared his throat. "What do you think about coming down here and helping out? Joel, Jeff, and Craig are all here," he said, naming his business partners. "We are fully staffed, but we are still slammed. Kennedy is coming down to help too. Hillary is going to watch the baby. Chase has too many fares, so he's out driving. But we could really use a hand."

Paige stood from her exercise ball and started for her bedroom. "What's going on? Why are you so busy?"

"We overbooked food trucks, so we have three of them here. They're super popular on social media and they drew a crowd. There was some college football game up the road too, and—" he stopped talking to her and had an exchange with someone else before coming back to their conversation. "Anyway, what do you say? Can you come help out?"

Paige wasn't one to turn down work, especially if it was that busy. Tips would be plentiful. "I'll be there in twenty."

"You're the best, Paige. Love ya!" he shouted as he disconnected the call.

Paige looked down at the blank screen. *Love ya!* The words still resonated in her ear, but humored her all the same. He was a good pal, that's all there was to it.

MEET THE AUTHOR

Bestselling Author Bernadette Marie is known for building families readers want to be part of. Her series The Keller Family has graced bestseller charts since its release in 2011. Since then she has authored and published over forty books. The married mother of five sons promises romances with a *Happily Ever After always*... and says she can write it because she lives it.

Obsessed with the art of writing and the business of publishing, chronic entrepreneur Bernadette Marie established her own publishing house, 5 Prince Publishing, in 2011 to bring her own work to market as well as offer an opportunity for fresh voices in fiction to find a home as well. Bernadette is also an educator in the industry, offering workshops and speaking at conferences. In 2020 she was named the Independent Writer of the Year from the Rocky Mountain Fiction Writers.

When not immersed in the writing/publishing world, Bernadette Marie and her husband are shuffling their five hockey playing boys around town to practices and games as well as running their family business. She is a lover of a good stout craft beer and might be slightly addicted to chocolate.

Other Titles from 5 Prince Publishing
www.5princebooks.com